O9-AIG-215

# Indelicacy
## A Novel

# Amina Cain

---

**A ghostly feminist fable about finding the freedom to live as one desires**

In "a strangely ageless world somewhere between Emily Dickinson and David Lynch" (Blake Butler), a cleaning woman at a museum of art nurtures aspirations to do more than simply dust the paintings that surround her. She dreams of having the liberty to explore them in writing, and so must find a way to win herself the security and time to use her mind. She escapes her lot by marrying a rich man sympathetic to her "hobby," but having gained a husband, a house, high society, and a maid, she finds that her new life of privilege is no less constrained. Not only has she taken up different forms of time-consuming labor—social and erotic—but she is now, however passively, forcing other women to clean up after *her*. Perhaps a more drastic solution is necessary?

Reminiscent of a lost Victorian classic in miniature, yet taking equal inspiration from such modern authors as Jean Rhys, Octavia Butler, Clarice Lispector, and Jean Genet, Amina Cain's *Indelicacy* is at once a ghost story without a ghost, a fable without a moral, and a down-to-earth investigation of the barriers faced by women in both life and literature. It is a novel about seeing, class, desire, anxiety, pleasure, friendship, and the battle to find one's true calling.

**Amina Cain** is the author of two collections of short fiction, *Creature* and *I Go to Some Hollow*. Her essays and short stories have appeared in *n+1*, *The Paris Review Daily*, *BOMB*, *Full Stop*, *Vice*, the *Believer Logger*, and elsewhere. She lives in Los Angeles and is a contributing editor at *BOMB*.

**Farrar, Straus and Giroux | 2/11/2020**
9780374148379 | $25.00
Hardcover with dust jacket | 176 pages
Carton Qty: 28 | 7.5 in H | 5 in W
Brit., 1st ser., audio: FSG
Trans., dram.: Janklow & Nesbit Associates

**ALSO BY AMINA CAIN**

*I Go to Some Hollow*

*Creature*

# INDELICACY

# AMINA CAIN

## INDELICACY

FARRAR,
STRAUS
AND
GIROUX
*New York*

Farrar, Straus and Giroux
120 Broadway, New York 10271

Copyright © 2020 by Amina Cain
All rights reserved
Printed in the United States of America
First edition, 2020

Permissions tk

Library of Congress Cataloging-in-Publication Data
ISBN: 978-0-374-14837-9

Designed by Richard Oriolo

Our books may be purchased in bulk for promotional,
educational, or business use. Please contact your local bookseller
or the Macmillan Corporate and Premium Sales Department
at 1–800-221-7945, extension 5442, or by e-mail at
MacmillanSpecialMarkets@macmillan.com.

www.fsgbooks.com
www.twitter.com/fsgbooks · www.facebook.com/fsgbooks

1 3 5 7 9 10 8 6 4 2

*To Alex*

It's as if something that should happen is
waiting for me . . . it's something that owes itself
to me, it looks like me, it's almost myself. But it
never gets close. You can call it fate if you want.
Because I've tried to go out and meet it.

—Clarice Lispector, *The Apple in the Dark*

INDELICACY

I THOUGHT THAT BEING in the country would help me write, with its fields and its horses, but I don't think I was meant for that. For the country, or for help.

Out in the street, candles light every window. When I can't get my thoughts down, I look at them. The flames remind me of my future; I'm afraid I might burn everything up. People are walking in and out of the same four shops; I know they haven't bought anything good. When I went inside those shops, I was bored. I'm bored by this one street.

If something flows through me, I think it is mine. It is not mine. The carriages driving close to my windows.

It's strange being alone again. In the afternoons there's

a spaciousness larger than I've ever wanted. I had a husband and I left him; I wonder how he is. Now I have writing, but I also have too much of my own self. I am stalking my own soul.

I wanted to write about paintings, but I wasn't seen as someone who could say something interesting about art. I wasn't seen as someone who could say anything at all and then publish it. When I went with my husband to the museum, I felt I should be cleaning that place. I was used to that work and maybe it is my destiny. Before meeting my husband, I had mopped the floors of those galleries, over and over. I had scrubbed the walls until my palms were rough and dry.

I both liked and disliked going to work. When I was supposed to be cleaning, I would look out the windows of the museum, the paintings behind me reflected in the glass. It meant something to me to see myself with them. Never before had I thought paintings would be important.

I was learning how to be another. I would stand in front of the window for a long time, a bucket of water by my side. I watched the rain falling on the grass; at first, standing there, I hadn't even known it was raining.

My husband felt he was rescuing me, and in many ways he was.

I was told by my husband I was writing about my own mind. I was told this wasn't becoming. But I saw myself in the paintings; I saw everything there.

After my husband and I married, I had to open our house to guests—constantly. I had to entertain and I am not a good entertainer. At first I liked my new life. My husband bought me expensive dresses, and then more dresses. For the first time I wore gold. I had a writing room—that's not what my husband called it—and someone to bring me hot tea and coffee.

It's not only that my husband believed women couldn't write—it's that he didn't believe *I* could. My coming up in the world was in marrying him and in my new clothes and jewelry. It's true I did want everything he gave me, but I will die if I can't write and then I will have wasted my life.

I see myself then, a figure in the street, walking to the museum. To look out from my window and see myself like that. Moving in and out of experience.

But here is my own body, and my own chair. Here are my wrists. Sitting at my desk, I feel loving toward my wrists. I've made them do too much.

THE CLICK-CLACK OF SHOES and Antoinette appeared, the hallway dark behind her. "I was in the gallery with the armor," she said, "and I thought I heard something, but I always think that."

"It's awful in there. I usually hear things coming from the vents."

"I don't like when it's my turn to clean it."

"Help me here, and then we'll do that room together."

Antoinette dusted, barely, while I finished my mopping. "My dress is ugly," she said, sighing, looking at herself in the large windows. I don't think she ever looked at the art.

"No one's here to see you."

"When I walk home, they'll see it."

"Then you'll be wearing your coat. You'll be covered up."

She started to dust again. Then stopped. "We shouldn't have to wear ugly things."

The truth was that sometimes, if it wasn't freezing, I didn't even wear my coat in winter I was so ashamed of it, but I didn't say this to Antoinette; I didn't want to give her ideas, wrong ones. There were people who had no coat at all, who instead had to pile on shirts and sweaters.

"I want a husband," she said again out of nowhere.

"You'll have one."

"Yes, but he'll be poor and he'll wear an ugly suit."

"You'll love him anyway."

"No, I won't."

"I don't care if I marry," I said. "I want to write."

When we finished our cleaning, we went out into the evening and it was a relief, to be done with work and going wherever we chose. Antoinette didn't have the same freedoms I did—she lived with her family still—but she walked with me for a while. Out on the street we were both different; I felt connected to something around us, something good, though I don't know if I could say or even describe what that was. I could sense it all the same. I could sense an interaction. In the buildings and in Antoinette, her shoulder to her hand. Even in her face. The back of her head as she looked out at the city. The front and back of my own head too.

At a corner we stopped to watch a puppet show. There were young mothers with their children, and the puppets were colorful animals, more colorful than real animals would be. A bright mouse. A golden cat coming after it.

"I like the mouse," I said, though I wasn't a child.

"I wish my brother were here," Antoinette said. "He'd like it too."

"How old is your brother?"

"Six."

To be six, I could hardly picture it now. I had tried to block out a good bit of my childhood.

But this wasn't about me, it was about Antoinette's young brother, and I was always returning the subject to myself.

A T HOME THERE WERE the doorways of the other apartments, my own doorway swept clean. A song was in my mind, one I had heard in a shop I had gone into. I didn't know why it was accompanying me. A young woman had begun to play it right when I walked in, a cheerful harpsichord, or was it melancholy?

Maybe it is unbelievable, but I liked where I lived; another person might find it wanting. My rooms were small with hardly any furniture, but what was there was nice enough, if simple, and I kept it neat as a pin. A bedroom with a bed and a blanket. In the kitchen, a table and two sturdy chairs. I tried to write at that table every night. I didn't think it was good. Still, I enjoyed it. The house where I had grown up was crowded with babies and yelling. Imagine being on your own after that.

After dinner I sat down to write and saw an image in my mind: three women in long white dresses playing catch with a skull. Dull afternoon there among the green firs. I don't know why it appeared to me; I couldn't remember ever seeing it in the museum.

Often when I went to bed at night and closed my eyes: paintings. The way waves must appear when you close your eyes at night if you've been to the beach. Or I saw my notebook, sturdy black with white pages, and what I had put down that day.

The first part I had written in pencil, sitting outside in the sun. Then as it got darker, I wrote something else. Then I didn't write at all. I felt proud because something outside my mind had brought me there. It wasn't my energy I was responding to.

Sometimes I saw what I had read:

*My needle is sticky, and it creaks as it goes in and out of the canvas. "My needle is swearing," I whisper to Louise, who sits next to me. We are cross-stitching silk roses on a pale background. We can color the roses as we choose, and mine are green, blue, and purple. Underneath, I will write my name in fire red . . .*

Antoinette was right. We terrified the rich. The waves of people arriving in the morning and leaving late evening, I tried to be a part of that energy but it wasn't possible. My dresses rough and plain to match all the roughness about me.

I would buy myself something, a pretty new blouse or a pair of red stockings, even if I had to skip lunch for a week to afford it. Maybe I would also buy myself a book. Each thing would give me a different kind of pleasure. I would read the book in my bed at night.

IN THE MORNING I WALKED TO WORK AGAIN. The river was two streets over, and once in a while I caught a glimpse of it, or I caught a glimpse of the air just above. In front of the museum a line of people wrapped around the corner of the building, the women in their full skirts.

Here was a woman in a stunning emerald dress, a white feather sticking out of her hat like a warning.

Inside the museum, another woman looked at a painting of a witches' Sabbath, the figures on the canvas huddled together, their bodies forming the shape of an oval. Light was on the woman's face, her cheeks flushed.

I had to mop the bathrooms. I had to scrub the toilets and the sinks. It was the worst part of my job and I didn't know how to do it without wanting to throw my bucket of water on someone.

This woman who looked as if she'd rather be sewing, she kept taking her embroidery out. She left her husband to wander the galleries while she sat on a bench in the lobby, working steadily on a piece of pale blue cloth. I wanted to throw my bucket of water on her.

E VERY MORNING AND NIGHT I walked through that city, to and from the museum, fall turning into winter. Each doorway, even mine, its own theater of something, with its own suggestion or promise.

I allowed myself to go into clothing shops, and when I found a delicate black blouse I thought would go well with a simple skirt, and when I had saved enough money, I allowed myself to buy it. Trying it on in the dressing room, I became different. I left the shop, the small bag tucked under my arm. I don't think I looked different to anyone else, but I carried the bag proudly with me.

After work, if Antoinette came too, we would find ourselves walking next to the cold black river, following it to the black lake, sometimes stopping to throw crumbs for the birds. Two figures on a canvas. I saw us in that way.

"I want a bathing suit," she said one evening. I don't like to hear a person's voice during this kind of moment.

Then we walked again. At a market we bought hot chocolate and drank it while sitting on a bench in front of the lake. Other people sat on other benches and the air was chilly. We were anything but alone. This time I didn't mind listening to the things she wanted: a one-piece, backless bathing suit, a silk dress, a gold necklace with stars on it, a turquoise blouse. A portrait of her desires, there at the lake with the waves rising gently up in the darkness. I wanted her to have all of it.

"Can you imagine," she said dreamily, "a party in which you receive all the things you've wanted all year, and then you put them on one by one?"

"To be honest, I can only imagine receiving one of them."

"Why only one?"

"I try to imagine things that might actually happen. It's more pleasurable that way."

"None of it will come true, so what does it matter?"

"You're right, and yet . . ."

I would get her the blouse. After all, I had just saved enough for my own, why shouldn't I get one for Antoinette? A few more skipped meals and I would be able to afford it.

FOR A WHILE, then, my breaks at the museum were spent in the galleries. If I couldn't eat, at least I would see something nice. I would write about it. One of the drawings I liked most was *Three Virtues*, and I went to it often. I would sit on the bench facing the drawing and forget where I was. Three different figures of a man fading into a red background while I faded into the room. It was certainly a strange drawing, though I don't think it was meant to be. Sometimes I looked at pages from the Quran, studying its lettering. But I knew I was different from the other museumgoers; I had my work to do. Only when I was walking or at home could I be myself.

I wrote down my descriptions of the paintings, my notes, but I wasn't sure what I would do with them. *The Trojan Women Setting Fire to Their Fleet, The Annunciation, Margaretha van Haexbergen.*

Then I would see Antoinette, looking at herself in the mirror in the bathroom, careless, her sponge on the floor. In the courtyard in her—it was true—ugly coat. I started to write descriptions of her, the things she did when she was supposed to be cleaning, the way she looked when she spoke or was silent. I liked doing this as much as I liked describing the paintings, but I didn't tell her I was doing it. I didn't talk about writing at all. She continued to tell me the things she wanted, that she had seen in the shops. Sometimes I wrote these things down in my notebook too. In my mind I began to picture her in the clothes she wanted, as if the intensity of her desire had made them appear. Very clearly, I saw her in a maroon dress.

TODAY AS ANTOINETTE *and I were leaving the museum, we stopped to look at a painting of Mary. Or maybe it was me who looked; Antoinette was restless. In this painting, Mary is lying down but she's awake to something. She's looking up, her eyes open just enough to see what's in front of her, or perhaps what she's seeing is inside her own mind. Her white robe is slipping from her shoulders, her hands clasped, her arms resting on her pregnant belly. A red blanket. A dark room. It must be cold outside. Inside too. She is lit not radiantly, but with a half radiance and shadows all around. They touch her. And the red blanket gives off warmth, but Mary's skin also looks warm. She appears as if she's in ecstasy. I wonder what it feels like.*

ANTOINETTE VISITED ME at my apartment only once. She came over and I made us mint tea. We each ate an orange. A biscuit.

"You have hardly any furniture," she said in surprise.

"I have enough."

She looked around. "Hardly anything at all."

It was true, but the things I liked were around me. Lying on my bed and waiting for me to return to it was a novel about a poet. An autumn leaf sat on the table between us, Antoinette in one chair and me in the other. We drank our tea.

"Someday I hope to have a parlor with very beautiful furniture in it," she said. "I would spend all of my time there. A place to relax when I am not out visiting and a place to entertain my own guests. Wouldn't you like that?"

"I'm not sure."

"The parlor or the visiting?"

"Both, but especially the visiting." Antoinette appeared

hurt. "I don't mean you. This is different. I consider you to be my friend and so it's my pleasure to have you here."

"Do you really think of me as a friend?"

"Of course. And me? Do you see me as a friend?"

"Yes," she said shyly.

"Go on. What would the parlor look like?"

"The wallpaper would be navy blue with orange flowers on it." She stopped and thought awhile. "A magenta-and-black Turkish rug in the shape of an oval would sit in front of the sofa. I don't know what color the sofa would be."

"Something neutral," I offered.

"Gray."

Though we had only dirtied a few dishes, and she always tried to clean as little as possible at work, Antoinette insisted on washing them before she went. It was sweet and I began to love her then.

CLOSE TO CHRISTMAS, there was chamber music in the front room of the museum. Before the concert began, the audience took their seats and then the musicians did. The instruments were taken up. There was the violin, filling the room. The lights from the windows shone out into the snow.

This was my first concert. I was able to see Antoinette's parlor. The oval rug.

While I dusted, I listened to the music and afterward wanted to describe it in my notebook. I was thinking things that I was afraid I would forget. Also, I had become interested in my handwriting. I wanted to see it there, in its own way, alive.

Antoinette's handwriting, I had begun to see it written across her face. What she wanted, in cursive.

But I did my cleaning. The toilets sparkled afterward. I scrubbed the walls. They were constantly, constantly dirty.

Then I walked home enjoying my evening, still hearing

that music in my head. A green wreath made of bay leaves hung in the center of a door. Next to it, a stack of wood gathered for a fire. There was the shop with a blouse for Antoinette. I could already picture her in it, eating dinner with her future husband at a nice restaurant. Sitting in the botanical gardens in the domed greenhouse, the windows frosted over in ice.

When I was at home for the night, I sat in my bathtub in water as hot as I could stand it and read for as long as I could.

In books I found even more strongly my desire to write, to write back to them and their jagged, perfect words. I found life that ran close to my own.

I don't think Antoinette had time to read; I don't think she had time for anything, and maybe that was why she was so lazy at the museum. When she wasn't working, she had to take care of her brother and sister, for her mother, who was sick, for her father, already dead.

I tried not to remember my own family. Away from them I had found my freedom, a space to think. I would clean my rooms with tenderness (I still couldn't believe they were mine alone) and then sit down again at my table. There was nothing to block me from it. The relief of reading and of being alone. The relief of trying to write.

Every day I did my dreaming, but as usual I forced

myself to do it practically, to imagine not that I would be a known writer whom many people read, but that I would publish one book at the end of my life. I knew that even this would make me happy. And I knew how lucky I was; I could have had to work at a glue factory.

ONE NIGHT THAT SEASON I woke suddenly, my stomach nervous. I sat up, and when I looked around, I saw the walls were empty: not a single thing. The windows were enough, I had always thought, but Antoinette had again been right. Now I wanted something warm. I pictured the autumn leaf on my table, its brown veins, my own veins blue, the length of my arm.

I didn't know where the nervousness might be coming from, so I sat at my table, a blanket around me, and I wrote with some anxiousness in the middle of the night. I tried to go right into it because I thought I might be able to come out on another side.

*The people in the painting are huddled together as if for protection, as if freezing cold. Only some of the figures are distinguishable; the rest form a mass, that strange oval. They seem to be looking upon the devil with fear, not exhilaration or worship. The ones with their mouths open appear shocked or perhaps they are screaming. Some of them are wearing bandages on their faces; only their eyes peer out, white points of astonishment. One figure appears peace-*

*ful*—*a young woman who sits on a chair while everyone else is on the ground. She wears a muff on her hands and her face is soft, though her eyes you cannot see.*

There I was, a single candle in front of me; nervousness was new. Now I am used to it. I think it must surround me, everyone able to see it, the way I am able to see what surrounds them.

Back in bed, when I couldn't write anymore, I read aloud from a book to try to settle into a different feeling, a different kind of thought.

*It's my pleasure,* I heard myself say in my mind. *I consider you my friend.*

CHRISTMAS CAME and on Christmas Eve I gave Antoinette her present, which I had wrapped in pretty paper. We had just finished working for the night, our cleaning things put away and arranged neatly in the supply closet.

"But there's nothing for you," she said, surprised.

"I don't want anything."

"Oh my God," she cried, when she saw what it was. "Did you steal it?"

"Of course not."

"How did you afford it, then?" She seemed unsure of what to do, if she should accept it, but she held the blouse up to herself and asked, "How do I look?"

Outside the museum, the streets were full of people. Some of them were lining up for Christmas Eve mass in front of the cathedral, talking loudly, dressed in their church clothes. Others were going in and out of the shops. When I was young, my parents had taken us to a church that was small and drafty; I had always felt I was sitting outside. The colorful wall hangings had scripture on them. Women and men stayed on opposite sides of the room. It's not that the church was bad, but I wasn't meant to spend my life there.

Antoinette and I went to a restaurant, warm and bright, and ordered dumplings and borscht. It was the first time we had eaten together in a place like this, and while we waited for our meal, we sat a bit awkwardly together. But a candle was burning at our table, and every other table too, and I focused on it to steady myself.

*A cucumber, melons, butter lettuce, an apple. Why is what we have left on a table worthy of being painted? No matter. It waits for our return, for when we will take it up again. Now I will eat once more.*

"Are you comfortable?" I asked Antoinette.

"Not completely."

We smiled at each other.

"I feel more comfortable looking at restaurants than sitting in them," I said.

"I know what you mean."

But when we started to eat, something came over me and I relaxed and even became confident. I didn't care anymore if anyone looked at us; I didn't care what people might have seen in our faces, or in how we sat in our chairs. I was sure some of them sat in their own chairs quite conceitedly, as if they were meant for restaurants like this.

Antoinette ate her food carefully, in small bites, and this made me want to eat like a pig.

THE NEXT MORNING I awoke well rested, ready to spend the day working at my table. A great deal was written in my notebook and I wanted to think about what it meant. I wanted to go further into what I had written, but I didn't yet know how to do it. The words sat there so innocently. Other words were still meant to surround them.

I fixed my black tea and oatmeal. When the dishes were washed, I sat down again with my thoughts. I can't write when things are dirty, when things are scattered around. I need everything to be clear. I need them to be clean.

I can't say I wrote well, but I put down my words and phrases all the same, well into the afternoon. So different from any Christmas I had spent before. For one thing, I was alone. Without trying to, I saw those Christmases past, chopping carrots for my mother, chopping onions, my face a blank. Sitting around the table, so much larger than this one, so much messier.

*The woman in the painting is holding a book in pink-*

*and-gold cloth. France is behind her. Round trees and then mountains are seen through the open window. I want France to be behind me too.*

It began to snow. As I watched from my window, I felt it might carry me somewhere different, at least inside my mind. It did, yet I read what I had written and I knew it was stupid. The snow had not changed my writing or anything else.

Maybe I was writing only a commonplace book. Maybe what I thought and said was most suited for the dump.

I didn't want to clean the same things my whole life. I didn't want to clean at all. But if that is what I was meant for?

I thought and wrote and by evening I had only managed a single good paragraph. Another person would have written five pages. But I liked that paragraph and that gave me hope.

And maybe more important, I began to feel that I could see my writing—not the words or the paintings— somehow in between. That I had made a new thing.

I CONTINUED LIKE THIS and soon it was the last day of the year. I had to work, but I felt a sense of something else. I wondered what the New Year would bring me.

I mopped and then ate my lunch outside, even though it was windy and the leaves were falling from the trees; now they were dead. It looked as if it might snow again, but it didn't.

Before I had finished my soup, an older man came and sat near me. He wasn't eating; he appeared to be doing nothing at all. He looked at me, then looked again. Men looking at women like that are truly horrible. Especially when they are so much older, when they are nearly dead themselves.

After that, the winter dragged itself through its January, its February, its March, with its dirty snow and frozen mud. I felt I was dragging myself through as well. I hated March more than any other month, with its promises of warmth that never came.

My writing was not unlike that. I would write, then read out loud what I had written and realize I was not any closer to a book than I had ever been. I began to hate writing, though I also still loved it.

I thought if I spent time in the country every day I would be able to write. Walk in the morning, write in the afternoon, walk again in the evening, then write again. Late at night, read. Then write again. Sleep.

One day I looked for a while at a small painting and saw something in it. A man and a boy in muted suits doing their engraving work, the background behind them completely dark. *We are not meant to see anything beyond this task, their concentration on it. Yet we want to know, it is only a scrap. What is in the darkness?*

This was my slogging through. Until spring came.

HERE IN THE COUNTRY I look at children's books when I go to the library because there are no good novels. There are no good books of art. If I'm honest, I'm comforted by their illustrations; something in them reaches me.

It rains in a drawing, and if the drawing is good, you feel wet. The hard rain falls on the umbrellas moving slowly down the street.

Maybe I have always needed things to be softened, as things are softened for children. If I were honest about who I am more of the time, I would write more honest things.

When I was younger, I felt everything around me;

one summer this was especially true. It sounds simple, but it was because the town where I lived was empty. I can't say why the emptiness was so nice; maybe because normally so many people were everywhere. When they were gone for the summer, that emptiness made space for me. I was aware of my future, and I could also relate to myself as a child. That was when I was fourteen.

But I take my evening walks here now. I begin just as it is getting dark and then walk into that darkness. It is the best time. The plants are hard to see, but sometimes a leaf or a flower is glowing in a bit of light from the window of a farmhouse. The scent of the flowers is more refreshing then, not heavy with the day, and the day's sun.

Everything in this house is warm right now: the hand soap, the towel, me. Even the fan blows warm air here in this country summer.

I T'S STRANGE MY HUSBAND NOTICED ME, but he came to the museum to see the paintings of Caravaggio and then of Goya, and the third time I was mopping the floor of the coatroom when he came for his jacket and umbrella. We stood together near the coats for some time, talking, and then he walked me home.

"Aren't you embarrassed?" I asked, and he said he was never embarrassed by anything.

We were married at the start of summer and hardly anyone attended—a few of his friends, a cousin from Brazil. No one I knew was there. While our vows were being said, I looked at him and wondered, *Who are you?* I thought I could see something different in him that I had never seen in someone else with money, and this made me feel comfortable.

I didn't tell Antoinette. I didn't even say goodbye.

I don't know how it was possible, but I felt natural in the rooms of my husband's house, and I walked around feeling that they were mine. Even when I saw them from the outside, the tall windows, curtains drawn, the rooms lit beautifully. I liked looking at them, knowing I could go in.

At first my husband wanted to have sex all the time. I liked being naked in our bed. When I had to get dressed to entertain, I was resentful. I wanted to tell our guests that I had just had sex with my husband, but things are more formal than that. I wanted to sit quietly in front of the window as the cat did. I wanted to show my excitement like the dog.

Life went normally, I guess. In the mornings when my husband got up, I got up too, though there was nowhere I had to be going. My husband would kiss me goodbye, then from the window I would watch him leave. I didn't feel I could go look at paintings; I was much too sheepish for that. I would see Antoinette.

I should have been honest with her. I felt it would be crushing, though maybe it would have given her hope, that I had found a rich husband, that things could change. But how would it have been for her to see me in my dresses, a newly wealthy woman?

I couldn't go to the market because I wasn't someone who did her own shopping, though I think I would have liked it, now that I had money to choose what I wanted. I had never had the opportunity to look at a nice loaf of bread, for instance, and say to myself, *I will get it.* But it appeared now in the house. Everything appeared there.

I wouldn't have to clean anything, and this was a relief, but I also felt guilty watching another person tidy up after me. I'm sure Solange didn't enjoy cleaning our toilets, as I also hadn't enjoyed cleaning toilets, but maybe she was at least happy to have a job, as I had been. My husband was nice enough, and to be honest, I wondered why he hadn't simply married her. She was beautiful and he was handsome and obviously didn't mind marrying beneath him. It would have been more convenient than marrying me, but I suppose people do not marry their own maids. And perhaps he had been able to see my ambition, however abstractly, and found it attractive. But when I told him I wanted to be a writer, he tried to persuade me otherwise.

"You don't have to prove anything," he said over dinner, some kind of fancy stew. "You've been working since you were twelve. Try to enjoy yourself."

The sound of my fork on my plate was loud. I made it louder. Now I was eating a salad. "I am trying to enjoy myself."

"Well, then try to relax."

"I'm afraid I'll get bored."

"Then get bored. You deserve it."

I had never felt I deserved anything, and if I was to begin, I couldn't start here. Still, I ate my stew. I ate my salad. In a way no one would have predicted, I began to consume my husband, but it would be a long time before either of us understood any of that.

I WROTE, THEN, when my husband wasn't at home, and sometimes I was able to do so for several hours, but then inevitably someone would arrive, some other young woman, and I would have to force myself to talk to her. "It's so delightful to have you here," etc. Unconsciously, I would see Antoinette's face transposed where the other face was meant to be. Or I would think back to a book I had been reading earlier that morning, and then—"Are you even listening?" The question was inevitable.

"Of course. It's just that I started to feel a headache all of the sudden, a migraine."

A migraine. Sometimes I had a sore throat. Or cramps. Then, excused from the visit, I would try to work again in my writing room.

Or I would go to the library to find novels to bring home with me, as I had before, though my husband insisted I buy any book I wanted.

I bought the ones I loved best, on orphans and ghosts and maids and revolutionaries, and I stacked them on top of the desk I was supposed to use to write letters, but that I used instead to write to myself. It still helped to be around those other books, to see the work of writing. I'm sure my husband would have found my book choices strange, but he never looked at them; I could read whatever I wanted.

From the outset, I thought I would like to be friends with Solange, but she kept herself protected from me; at least it felt like a kind of protection. I couldn't get her to talk in any way other than submissive. I tried speaking with her after breakfast, for instance, but it never went well. She only wanted to discuss the menu, what we would be needing for our meals in the week ahead.

"Do you like it here, Solange?" I asked.

She answered that she liked it very much. This was puzzling.

"Where is your family?" I tried again.

"I'd rather not talk about them, madame."

"You don't have to call me that, Solange. You see, I—"

"I should get the washing done now. There is really so much of it."

She hurried off. You see why I couldn't be friends with her; she never gave me the chance.

WHEN I COULDN'T WAIT ANY LONGER, I went to the museum. I wanted to see Antoinette and I wanted to look at the paintings; it had been almost six months since I was last there. Again it was Christmas and I walked the route from where I now lived feeling nostalgic for the year before, for that other route. It's not that I wanted to return to it exactly.

There was the music, there was the light shining out into the snow, there were the paintings and drawings. I had brought my notebook, I had worn my plainest dress, and I walked through the galleries looking for Antoinette. In every room I thought I might find her, but every room was empty.

I began going to the museum regularly and wrote again my descriptions of the things I saw there. I wrote about *Seven Works of Mercy* and *Portrait of a Woman as Saint Agnes*, and I still didn't know what I would do with these descriptions, what their purpose was, but filling the pages of my book was satisfying. I felt I must be filling myself too.

The more often I visited without catching a glimpse of Antoinette, the more I missed her, but I was afraid to make my inquiries, to enter the part of the museum for the people who worked there. I saw other young women scrubbing the walls or mopping, a few I remembered, but whom I had never gotten to know. We didn't say anything to each other.

I thought back to a night that previous winter, when in our wandering Antoinette and I had discovered a small tavern tucked in next to the lake and dared each other to go in. It had been foggy on the lake that night and so it felt as if one side of us were a void. *Be yourself again.* Inside, the tavern looked like a country inn, everything in wood, the walls and the floors, and at a long wooden bar sat many men. We wanted to get drunk, but we couldn't afford to. Sharing a single glass of something cheap, we listened to the music of a band playing in the corner. It too was all men; still, it was good. Someone was playing a fiddle.

"May I have this dance?" Antoinette asked, surprising me.

We danced in that place that was like a country inn, only one other couple dancing with us. I held Antoinette's shoulder and waist, self-consciously as always, yet some other part of me was relaxed. We kept smiling at each other, laughing. It was almost as if we were in a play, and it's true that everyone was watching us. Most people will watch two women dancing together.

Now, without asking where Antoinette might be, I would never know how to find her; I didn't even know where she lived. She might as well be lost in that void. So finally I got up my nerve. I went to my old employer, and he told me coldly that she was gone, that she hadn't worked hard enough, and so they had had no choice but to let her go. Other girls wanted to work, and so they were.

Antoinette my dreamer. I should have known.

I tried to speak to my old employer even more coldly than he had spoken to me, but he was a tough match. "How unpleasing you are," I said. "Like a tooth that hasn't been brushed in years and is growing hair on it."

My walks around the city were for Antoinette then, with the hope I might see her, looking into shop windows, throwing crumbs for the birds.

L IFE WENT ON WITHOUT HER and I became the person I was when I was married to someone, when I lived with someone and shared a bed. I did things I had never done before, that I had always been curious about. I tried to talk about my feelings. I gave my husband oral sex. I attended a lecture given by a famous psychotherapist. I attended concerts and plays, keeping a list of all the performances in my notebook, and one evening my husband finally came home with tickets to the ballet. Weeks before that I had told him I wanted to go, but because it took so long for him to get them, I thought he had forgotten. I was happy; it would be my first time going to the ballet and I added it to my list. As Solange was getting ready for bed, we were getting ready to leave. She was even quieter that night than usual.

After my bath, I sat in front of my mirror and thought about death. I had begun to worry about it, though I didn't want to, especially not in a moment such as that one. I put on a red silk dress and pulled my hair back from my face with gold combs. I had a gold necklace with stars on it.

We walked to the theater in the warm spring night, and I felt we were already hearing the music though we were still blocks away. It was drawing me to it.

Once there, my husband talked to a boring couple he knew, and I instinctively looked around for Antoinette. The theater was full and noisy. I knew I wouldn't see her, but what if her luck had changed? Now I regretted even more not telling her of my marriage, not having said goodbye.

Still, I enjoyed myself. How could I not? Our seats were close to the front; we could watch everything closely. When the lights came up onstage, eight dancers appeared, dressed in black. At first they were still, then in twos they began moving. Even that first moment made my heart beat.

Then another dancer appeared, wearing the mask of a horse, her hair sticking out of the back of the mask like a mane.

After that I went to the ballet as often as I could, all that spring. I didn't tell my husband it helped me to write, that I was inspired by it. I told him only that I loved it, that I enjoyed dressing up at night and going out into the city, both of which were true.

There was the dancing, but the music too enchanted

me, and the sets, though flat, were also real. I wanted to go inside the wooden buildings meant to conjure the street of a village. I was there in that village, though I was also still in my seat, completely taken in, the way I was so often taken in by scenes in paintings.

I ASKED TO TAKE BALLET CLASSES. I had to ask my husband for everything, though he always said yes. So much of the time I was either taking my long walks or sitting still, and I wanted to feel my body doing something else. I liked the stretching more than anything else. The dancing itself was more about discipline than freedom, and I knew discipline already, I knew about long hours and repeating some action again and again. Still, I think it was good for me. I felt clearheaded during that period.

I would stand at the barre and do my turning. I would watch myself doing it in the mirror. I liked the instructions being called out while we listened to the music. I liked it aesthetically. The teacher's voice, the piano, the room itself, the other dancers looking at themselves in the mirror too. I had not seen this kind of radiance before and I made note of it and tried to describe it. The teacher was radiant too, though I was sure she was quite old. All of it made me want to write.

One morning in class the teacher paid me a compliment:

"You look like a dancer, even if you are always one step behind." I began to take pride in this. I was not at a point where I worried about having an ego. Then, when I went to the performances, my relationship to them was different. Still ecstatic, but with a calm sense that I belonged there, in the auditorium at night, with my thoughts and my writing. I understood something about ballet easily, and this caused me to change.

There wasn't much time for talking with the other students in the class, but sometimes when we were waiting for the teacher, or standing outside the studio on our breaks, we spoke about the class and how difficult it was.

"I think I sprained my ankle," one of the students said.

"You should put ice on it right away," I responded.

"My legs are sore," another student said.

"It means you have worked hard," I told her.

I especially liked talking to a student named Dana. I thought she should dance professionally. The teacher complimented her constantly, and then Dana seemed to concentrate even harder. She never smiled. But I did. I smiled at her concentration.

Once I saw her at the ballet, wearing a white dress, her hair soft. In class, it was always severe. From her seat in the audience she watched the performance with her same focus, the same seriousness.

I wanted to talk to Dana about dance and writing and

paintings and music, though I didn't know how to start a conversation like that. I didn't always find talking easy, and I had never spoken to anyone about these kinds of things before. How should I begin?

With each new pose, we took turns practicing for our teacher. In those moments I was nervous to be the only one being looked at, but it helped me to watch Dana. In her body I saw what ballet was supposed to look like, how the arm should be held, what the hand should do. And I liked having a class to go to. In the same way I had always enjoyed school, for instance, and my family had distracted me from it. No one cared I had homework; I was expected to take care of my siblings instead. When I tried to read, I was always interrupted, so I had to do it where my family couldn't find me. Under a tree that took me thirty minutes to walk to. If I had stayed in that town with them, I would never have written a single word.

Now, after every class, I went home and, if no one paid me a visit, wrote.

*Giant trees covered in snow. And then the background changes. Giant cakes.*

After I had written, I would sit in the garden enjoying the evening, the warm air. Solange preparing dinner, cooking sounds coming from the kitchen window, my husband not yet home from work. I would listen to a bird cry, or the cat and the dog scratching around. In those moments I felt like a giant ear.

ONE DAY IN CLASS I asked Dana if she would like to go to the ballet with me, and from that point on we often went together. It was much nicer than going with my husband, who never seemed to pay attention to it, or the other young women with whom I had sometimes been forced to go, those women with whom I was supposed to be friends, who looked constantly around the theater to see who was in attendance, who only clapped or stood up when everyone else did. I stood and clapped whenever I wanted.

Dana and I would meet outside the dance studio and walk the two blocks to the theater, and I would ask her about her dancing, about her life.

"I'm afraid it's too late," she said early on in our conversations. "I didn't start young enough."

"But you're so good," I insisted. "You should never stop, even if you marry."

She smiled, and it seemed as if a secret was in her smile. "I won't stop dancing, but I don't know how far I'll get."

"You have already gotten very far indeed." I took her hand and pressed it in my own.

I wanted to tell her about my writing, but I was afraid she would think I was exaggerating my relationship to it, that I was lying. After all, I wasn't a *real* writer, yet I wrote every day. Though I hadn't cleaned for a while, to say that I was a maid would probably have been a more accurate way to explain who I was.

As we walked, the auditorium came into view, across from the park. Colorful streamers hung from the windows in blues and yellows, fluttering in the light breeze.

*When I am here, I am like the streamers,* I thought. *I'm connected to something, but then I am also connected to something else. It is always like that. I am flowing toward it.*

T HE GREEN GRASS COMBINED *with the pink sky. A restaurant lit brightly. But the restaurant is one feeling, the grass another.*

I write this in my time in the country, in my time of country walks.

Soon after we were married, my husband took me to the desert. Solange came with us. We stayed in tents, and every morning we came out into the sun and looked at a date farm in the distance. Solange came out of her tent too. The farm reminded me of a setting for a novel; it was so mysterious. Who would live there? And we became its characters. What had brought us together?

I pulled my hair into a loose bun, but not as a dancer

would do it. At night the fronds of the date trees moved
up and down—they didn't move at all during the day. I
learned from them, learned how to carry myself in the
evenings. I was connected to that younger me, the one of
emptiness, and something of that was also in my walking.

You see, everything came to me in the evenings and I
wasn't doing anything, I wasn't writing, I was just learning how to walk differently, and how to live in a tent.
Hot springs were near us, with grass growing all around.
This was the only grass to see. My husband and I would
soak in the water, Solange nearby with our towels. Before, I had hardly known that places like this existed, and
now here I was, seeing them.

W HILE READING IN BED AT NIGHT, sometimes I could hear Solange moving about in her room. She was always doing something. Maybe that was her energy. More industrious than Antoinette, than me. More dedicated to something. My husband already sleeping, I would rise from our bed and sit next to the window, where the air outside made contact with the room.

On her days off, Solange got up early and was gone before we ourselves had risen. I wondered where she went but she never told us. She needn't have and I'm glad she never did. As much as I still wanted to know her, she still didn't want to know me.

When she got back in the evenings, she often cleaned

her own rooms. They were even cleaner than I had kept mine, and she didn't decorate them, not even a book or a leaf. She must have liked that emptiness too, or else for her the house felt the opposite of a home and so she didn't treat it as one. It was simply the place where she worked and unfortunately she also had to live there. Or she didn't want to leave a trace or an impression of her life.

Once in a while I would see her look longer than normal at my husband; I didn't know what that was about. Only rarely did I see her in repose, sitting in the garden with a newspaper in her lap, eating food sent to her by her family. I would watch her eat and then try to move my thoughts to something else, but sometimes they brought me back to her.

*A woman stands in a room facing away from the viewer. Her dress is black, with either a white apron or cord tied around her waist. We can't tell which, but it affects how we see her all the same. It gives her shape; it separates her from her surroundings, which is not always so. At the bottom of the painting, for instance, her dress blends into the shadows on the floor.*

*We see also her white neck, her brown hair pulled back from it; she is looking down, but not completely. Maybe she is reading a letter.*

*The room is almost bare, except for a chair she's stand-ing next to, in front of her a table, and beyond the table a* furnace. *Two white doors, closed, lead to other rooms, other feelings, or else a continuation of this one.*

*I am always fooled by these suggestions of other rooms we might go into, but never can, never will. Another space, but it is closed to us, even if it feels open. Thought of in a different way, if it is all suggestion, what is in the rooms is ours.*

THE WEATHER BECAME BEAUTIFUL. Hotter than any summer I had known. I was going to dance classes, the museum, the library, the ballet. I was writing, entertaining hardly at all, my husband gone safely to work, where he couldn't interfere with my days.

I would walk around the city feeling as if I were on an island. Some tropical place. Wearing a light blouse, a light skirt, my hair pulled back from my face or in a loose bun. Through the park, along the busy streets, the river, and then the lake, which was so large it looked more like an ocean. The botanical gardens. There I could look at the tropical plants. I could sit and write among their green, rubbery leaves. And the desert plants. Among the spikes that rose out of the cacti. The spikes that rose out of me.

Occasionally a man would walk by and ask what I was doing. "A menu for a dinner party," I would say. Or, "I am writing down my dreams." When too many men had walked by with this same question, or some version of it, I said, "Your face looks like the butt of a wolf and it's interfering with my concentration." I was a rich woman now; I could say these things.

Then I would walk again, in a trance from the heat. I would go into a shop I'd never been to, wanting to costume myself in something, having seen the costumes of ballerinas and of actresses. Dressed for another time, another place. Hidden behind their makeup, cloaked, inaccessible. The distance didn't bother me in the way it did with Solange; I was drawn to their mysteriousness. Solange was a wall.

As the weeks went on in this way, I became more and more decadent, or at least it felt like decadence. Not through money. Though if I am honest, I became decadent in that way too. But when I was at home, if I wasn't at my desk or eating a meal, I was lying down, the dog and the cat lying next to me. In the back garden, in the bedroom, even in the room where I wrote. What luxury to lie around like that.

I especially didn't want Solange to see me. What would she think I was doing, and would she resent me for it? My husband expected it of me, so I didn't have to feel self-conscious around him. He had wanted me to take it easy. That is what he had wanted most of all.

In some ways it was good for me, and useful. In this lying down I became another part of myself, the part that was more like a tropical bird, and this helped with my writing. This is what I was, what I am, if that part of me is still in existence.

But when I was that relaxed, I didn't think of Antoinette. A part of me was forgetting her.

I became addicted to my trances. I went into them so easily.

As I became more decadent, Dana became more serious. We were no longer in class together because I had stayed a beginner and she had become more advanced. But we still went to the ballet together, and sometimes she came to our house. We would sit in my writing room and I would ask Solange to bring food and she would bring it.

That summer, Dana told me about her life, and I began to tell her about mine. She narrated her childhood, how her sisters had found her odd and she had found them shallow. She told me how she discovered dance:

"I didn't think about it when I was younger. I liked going to the ballet with my family, but it didn't occur to me I might want to be onstage too. I knew there was something I should be doing and that I was incomplete not doing it, but I thought I had time to figure it out, and it was exciting to have something like that to uncover. I took an acting class and at first I liked it, but I didn't truly belong. I didn't want to talk all the time."

"I wanted to write, always," I blurted out. I could not stop myself from saying this.

"Then we've both found what makes us happy."

"We have. Isn't that amazing?"

A T THE END OF JULY my husband took me to the ocean, we were to have a vacation, and Dana arranged to go at the same time. She only had to convince her sisters and that was easy. They were bored in the city; they always saw the same men.

It became something, sitting together on a blanket in the sand, sisters looking for husbands, husband going off somewhere to work and joining me at night. Solange was on vacation too, but not with us. I didn't want someone to wait on me. I wanted to walk on the beach. I wanted to look at things in the distance, be faced with the water; I wanted to swim. I had never spent time at the ocean before. Finally I saw it at night when I closed my eyes to sleep.

Dana and I would swim out and look at the horizon and tread water. Later we'd come back to our towels and fall asleep on the sand. We put on our light dresses and talked. I told her about my writing and we went for ice cream and I felt I was in heaven.

One morning jellyfish were floating on the surface

of the water, white things taking their shape from the waves that washed under them, then becoming flat again when the sea became flat. We watched them for a while, fascinated, then Dana got impatient; she couldn't swim, so she wandered off and suddenly I had the day to myself.

I walked along the shore. I took a path that ran into a garden thick with palm trees and birds-of-paradise and hibiscus and jasmine. I had never seen plants like this, not quite in this way, not outside a greenhouse, and I added the experience to my list. The garden was so dense and the leaves of the plants as substantial and alive as the ocean itself. It was good to see that plants too could have such presence. I understood how drugs were made from them, how they might transport people or keep them alive.

Later I sat quietly in a restaurant and, while I waited for my lunch—it was past lunchtime and the restaurant was nearly empty—looked at the sea and wrote in my notebook. Only once or twice did I say exactly what I wanted, but I kept going regardless.

*The perspective of the painting is one of gazing at, not taking part in, a service. Where the viewer is there are no lights, not even a single candle. Where the people are worshipping, it is bright, though some stand partly in the shadows. You look at the painting and you want to go farther into the room; there is something comforting about both the light and the dark that draws you. And where there is light, it goes all the way up to the high ceilings. The inside of the chapel is pretty (it is a side chapel, not the main part of the church), with intricately carved wooden walls and columns; Gothic, but not heavily, with tall windows. The perfect place to be on a cold evening.*

All of the windows in the restaurant were open, and as I wrote, the waves were crashing right outside them. It began to help me. I began to feel I was in a trance of writing. All around me were plump insects. They too were very alive, beating their wings, landing.

THAT NIGHT I tied my husband to a chair. He always had sex the way I wanted; he didn't try to control it and he seemed to like that. It was one of the few things I had control of when it came to him and me.

If I were another kind of woman, maybe I wouldn't have let him out of my sight, but I let him out of my sight often. I was naturally out of his sight, as women usually are with their husbands. It gave me great freedom.

"Are you enjoying yourself?" he asked after I had untied him. The pleasant room was made for the tropics, with windows that lined every wall. So different from the rooms in our city; here we were always exposed to the outside, to the plants and the ocean. Or perhaps they were always exposed to us. Either way, they were part of the room.

"I've never felt so well."

"I want you to feel well."

"Do you?" I nuzzled into his arm. Some people always feel well. I suppose he is one of them.

"You're almost like an animal," he said. "I never know what you will do."

"I know."

A red squirrel climbing a tree.

"But in reality you're a woman."

I laughed. "What does that mean?"

"It isn't nice to call your wife an animal, is it?"

"I think it's interesting."

But then my husband was annoyed with me, for I had taken the conversation too far, even though I had hardly taken it far at all. "You try to make yourself abnormal on purpose," he said. "You think it makes you better than the other people around you."

"I do no such thing, and still I am better."

I knew how that sounded, but I couldn't help saying it, and I suppose I did think I was better than him. If I'm being honest. If I'm being shallow.

WITH HER SISTERS, Dana left before we did to begin her rehearsals. It would be her first performance and she was nervous. On the last day of her vacation, she stopped to look at a gray cat in an apartment window when we walked by it. Her hair was twisted into an elegant shape, pulled away from her brown neck, and I saw how striking she was as she looked at the cat.

The cat was striking too, the way it looked at us both in turn.

"Dana, it wants to communicate. It watches us as we watch it."

We got fancy doughnuts and ate them at a wooden table. I wasn't used to doughnuts and later felt sick to my stomach. Even at night I was nauseous, and while my husband went to a place where poker was played, I lay in bed feeling sorry for myself, the ocean again close to me, darkly crashing into the bright sand.

The next day I ate carefully. I didn't eat bread. I was careful about everything, even swimming. I didn't want to get sick again. Instead, I read a novel I had brought with me that I had barely touched since first arriving. I was able to enjoy myself in that way.

Soon we would leave too, back to the city. At least it would still be hot. I could still go to the botanical gardens, walk through the park in the evenings. I could go to the lake.

THE FUTURE CAME, as it always does, with its changes and its things that stay the same. Dana in *Giselle*, a small role. In her room, Solange was as quiet as always, though occasionally it sounded as if she was talking to someone, sometimes in a soothing way, yet I had never seen her be soothing. It seemed so out of character. To whom was she talking? My husband? No matter. I went to the library to look at books of botanical illustrations. There I found the plants I had seen at the ocean, their strange leaves, and flowers that were also sometimes strange, with a heavy presence, but not weighed down. Different from plants that died every winter.

To my husband it made sense that I would look at botanical illustrations. He didn't understand my relationship to the plants; he thought I was only interested in their flowers, that I might ask to plant some in our garden. Or maybe I'm wrong. Maybe he understood more than I imagined.

I wanted to write about the plants, but that seemed even harder than writing about paintings. When I tried,

I barely captured them. But every day I walked for a half hour to the library to look at the illustrations, then I went to the botanical gardens on my way home.

One Sunday I went to an afternoon performance of *Giselle* and watched Dana onstage. She danced as one of the dead women who have been betrayed by their lovers and will kill any man who crosses their path. All of these dead women were graceful, but in Dana was something mournful, perhaps without her knowing it was there. Is it bad to say she was better than those other dancers?

W HEN I ARRIVED AT HOME, my husband was still out and Solange was closing the curtains in the front room. I sat down in a chair; I rarely sat in the front room, as it was formal. I had worn a simple, pretty dress.

"Shall I turn on the lights?" Solange asked. "It'll be dark soon."

"I won't be long."

"Can I bring you something to eat or drink?"

"May I have some water?"

I drank my water. In my head I heard the music I'd heard that afternoon. I saw the country. I even saw it in that room.

"Did you have a nice time, madame?"

"Yes, it was lovely. Did you have a good day?"

"I prepared tomorrow's breakfast."

"Solange, do you like breakfast?"

"That's an odd question, madame."

"I like dinner. It's by candlelight and the food tastes better. Is that odd too?"

Why did I say these things? If I wasn't polite, I was

awkward. Was I myself an odd person? I looked at Solange's heart-shaped face to try to find something there. She had been nice to me for the first time, and I had ruined it.

Did Solange have friends? Good friends? I imagined her and another young woman cleaning together, whispering, doing whatever they wanted when the owner of the house wasn't home.

In another life I owned a farm; I saw this clearly. I spent my time trying to tell my life's story to a man who had recently killed his wife, only I didn't know he had killed her, and he was bored hearing my story. I let him stay on the farm for many months, working the land.

I saw Antoinette lounging in a tropical place like the one I myself had just been to. I saw her sitting in a chair among plants, having her portrait painted.

I saw Dana walking in a city with desertlike mountains next to it and then in a lush green field.

I DIDN'T WRITE FOR A MONTH; my mind was somewhere else. But I *was* writing a book; I knew that now.
I had been writing it for two years. The problem was that
it would make little sense to most people, and how would
that work out? Everyone always wants sense.

Writing is endless, what it allows you to consider.
What is in paintings is endless too. I picture one I used to
look at often in the museum. A white peacock is about to
attack another that is colorful.

But even without sense in my writing, and with this
endlessness, I was starting to become calm; outwardly,
at least. Now it was not unusual for me to be in some
interaction with another and in control of it. This had
never been my experience, and I watched it happen with
some pleasure, but I never let this pleasure show. Even
in mundane interactions I had something interesting to
say, or I made the interaction better. Dullness was still
everywhere. But there was fascination too.

It began to get cold again. Now when I took my walks,
the air was different. Clearer. Soon I'd be walking in the

near dark before supper, all of the lights coming on in the shops. The tables in front of the restaurants carried indoors until spring, the sidewalks again empty. All of the fascination *inside*, where the diners sat and talked and waited for their meals.

WHEN THE COLD SETTLED IN, I took a train to another city to visit a museum where a glass chandelier hung from the ceiling of each room. I hadn't been on a train—or to another city—for quite some time, and I looked out at the land racing by or I read the novel I had brought with me. Trees and rivers. Three or four times, a farm. I wondered what it would be like to live on one of them.

The city was smaller than the one I lived in, but it too was situated along the same lake my city was, and that is where I found its museum. When I stepped off the train, I spotted it right away, more modern than I had expected, a bright white next to the turquoise water. It felt nice to be somewhere new, to be there alone.

With only a few people walking through it, the museum was quiet. I could hear my footsteps on the hardwood floors and people talking quietly as they looked at the paintings. The museum in my city was loud. In the galleries here the paintings were large, but in a corridor were several small ones, two I felt especially drawn to, for they were flat in their style, and I had always been drawn to paintings like this. They appeared to be doubles, but when I looked closely, I noticed that they were different.

*Four figures are in the first painting: Jesus, the Virgin Mary, and two others, perhaps a priest and a nun. These figures look as though they are made of white clay; they're ugly. The Virgin Mary's face is the same color as her clothing. Jesus too, the same color as his loincloth. But the hills behind are green; they look as if they were flowing toward something, as an ocean does, and the roof of the cathedral in the distance is bright blue. In this painting the things that are not alive are much brighter than the ones that are living, who look as dead as the one who's been killed.*

*The second painting was done one hundred years after the first, and though it closely follows the original, it adds to the scene a new figure and softens the features of those who are present. Jesus is still dead, but the others finally look alive, and even Jesus has been given some color. The hills this time are brown and they are not flowing. In the first painting, it is the landscape that comforts, but in the second it is the people. The aliveness of the scene has been given back to the living.*

I focused on the paintings for a long while, until another museumgoer cleared his throat. I had been in front of the doubles for quite some time, and I suppose he wanted to look at them too. But these days I rarely conceded anything. This was when I learned selfishness, right after I had learned control. It's not that I became a selfish person, but I knew selfishness now and it would always be a part of me. If I walked by a shop window, I thought not only that I wanted what was inside, but that I deserved it. I felt I would look nice, that gold became me, that nice fabric became me. They become everyone, of course.

But I moved aside, went on to the next gallery. I looked at the lake through one of the windows of the museum, imagining Antoinette going to her own window, becoming visible to the people walking down the street. Visible to me. In her long, unfashionable skirt, her shirt sleeves rolled up to her elbows. She's carrying with her that other time. We all carry our lives in us, not just our problems or nightmares, but something of what we were before.

One by one we become visible, Antoinette. On the farm or in the city. In the museum or out on the street. I'm just as visible in my bedroom as I am anywhere else.

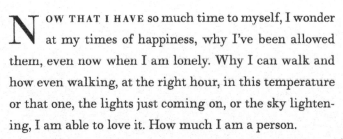

NOW THAT I HAVE so much time to myself, I wonder at my times of happiness, why I've been allowed them, even now when I am lonely. Why I can walk and how even walking, at the right hour, in this temperature or that one, the lights just coming on, or the sky lightening, I am able to love it. How much I am a person.

At home I would watch my husband pour himself a glass of water. When he went up the stairs, I could hear the rain falling all along the rooftop, along the windows. It rushed along the street.

Did I join with him, at least in certain moments? Did it mean something for us to live so closely to each other, even if I am now gone? All around us the buildings facing out at their corners, as though a person were always coming toward them. That is what the city seemed like then.

At first I thought I knew myself well.

Yet, what part of me is false?

I N DECEMBER, Dana turned twenty-one and her family threw her a birthday party. I went shopping for a new dress and I also looked at jewelry. I didn't need jewelry, it wasn't my birthday after all, but I wanted to look at it just the same. In a department store I saw earrings that looked like drops of blood and I wanted to wear them. I felt the earrings would make the rich people at the party kind to me, and that if I kept them my whole life, they would guard me against becoming poor again, against becoming a future hag, that all my nice things would guard me, even if it wasn't true.

Regardless, I wanted something and I could have it. It had been this way for a while.

So I bought a dress, a fitted dark-green-and-black one, and I bought the earrings, and I wore them to Dana's party with my husband on my arm. The house was decorated with globes of light and an excess of flowers. Conversationally it was less striking, as it almost always was. As for me, what I said out loud to the people at the party was completely different from what I was thinking. This is how it usually was. Still, I was able to be calm.

I had always thought I would be forced to marry an older man, but my husband was young, and his clothes fit as well as mine did. So some of the women disliked me, as they always did. But I also disliked them.

Dancers were at the party and to watch them eat was interesting. They did so differently from everyone else, more gracefully. I was not a graceful eater; there was still something piglike about me. They didn't drink goblets of wine, they had to stay composed, they had to give everything to their performances, and in the same way I wanted to give everything to my writing. I wanted people to see it in the way I ate things and acted. That eating was more than just eating, or that writing was. That friendship was, my friendship with Dana. A part of me wished I could announce our friendship at the party.

But I didn't. I did my socializing, my version of it, and when I did, I saw scenes of winter, I saw myself writing in the winter. I saw the frozen river running alongside our city. Always so distracted. Eventually, I excused my-self to fill my plate again.

"Are you having a good time?" Dana asked as I was spooning mashed potatoes next to a clump of spinach. I hadn't known she was near.

"Yes," I answered, surprised by my answer. In my own way I suppose I was. "Are you?"

"My mother is trying to introduce me to someone."

"Who?"

"Him." She pointed to a man.

"No."

Dana laughed and looked toward another guest. That guest was snorting something off a small plate. She looked pretty doing it and we watched her for a few moments.

In a sitting room outside the bathroom, another woman sat in front of a mirror and brushed her hair roughly, so roughly a real drop of blood was beginning to appear on her scalp.

I DIDN'T HIDE MY WRITING from my husband anymore, or even my study. I called it "my study" even
if he called it my sitting room, even if he glanced at
but said nothing about the pages on my desk, the books
crowded around them. Even Solange ignored my papers,
but then she rarely asked me anything. I don't think she
ever dusted off my desk, and she too insisted on using the
words *sitting room*. It is true I sat when I wrote, when I
read. And when Dana came over, we sat there too.

"Would you like to travel again?" my husband asked
one morning while I was dressing. He liked to watch me
do this, dress and undress. At such moments he always
seemed to appear.

"I want to go to Jamaica," I said.

I was putting on a burgundy dress, preparing for
writing and the walk I would take just after breakfast.
Preparing for my own mind. Why did I get so dressed up
when no one would see me? It is better that way, to give
fancy things to my writing and my own mind and my
ramblings, better than wasting them on people I don't

like, and their formal, grand rooms, while it snows outside. All of the fascination *out there*, away from where we are sitting.

But I felt then that I could also dress for the future, for when I would be in Jamaica. That I had become a worldly person and that everyone would be able to see this in how I dressed. That I was someone who traveled.

Finally my husband left for work; now I would have some space. I finished my morning routine and went down to the kitchen for breakfast. The animals followed me, the dog's nails clicking along the floor, the cat's silent walking.

"Sit down, madame," Solange said when I arrived in the kitchen.

On the table my oatmeal was waiting for me. My egg.

While Solange busied herself around me, I ate in silence. To eat something warm and without having to talk to anyone was nice.

I began writing in my mind. Gazing out the window but not seeing what was there.

I took my walk in much the same way, then in my study I wrote well into the afternoon without stopping, which was so rarely the case; I usually stopped quite often. When I had finished, the lights were starting to come on in the buildings opposite and I looked at them lovingly, seeing things this time. Life was happening everywhere; our bit of it was only a small contribution. Still, our lights joined the darkening of the sky, those other lights. I wanted this feeling to enter into what I was writing, but without saying it directly it was difficult to do.

That night I had a concert to go to. Finally I had gone to so many concerts I stopped taking note of them. A perfect end to a long day of writing, I thought, though the room in which the concert took place was cold and, in that way, annoying. I sat in the audience with the other concertgoers in a semicircle surrounding the musicians, we were close, and the entire time I cried. I hadn't expected it; this hadn't happened at any of the other concerts I had gone to. *Focus yourself,* I thought. *Stop crying.* But it was no use. Imagine being too close to the musicians in a moment like that. I didn't want my crying to disrupt them, but there was no way to stop it. Again, the music rose up to the ceiling and went out into the rest of the room. The violin was much more precise than I was or would ever be. Compared to it, I would always be dull and general. Still, it seemed to cut through something inside me and then soothe what it had cut.

The woman to my left looked at me anxiously. I was not crying loudly; still, I imagine it was disturbing, or at least a great distraction.

When the concert ended and we stood to leave, I was surprised I hadn't been kicked out. A few of the concertgoers smiled at me, especially the older ones. I was grateful for that. They pitied me, I suppose. Or they related to the moment. They had once felt it. Now the woman to my left wouldn't look at me at all.

Walking home, I noticed in a bare tree a huge nest, and for some reason it made me feel alone. But I was not alone, other people were walking everywhere. And I had a husband I was going home to. I had a good friend.

A ND THAT MEANT something, didn't it? For indeed I was a part of people's lives. They were a part of mine. In the middle of the winter, Dana's family went for a week to visit relatives in the country, but Dana had to stay home for her performances. I stayed with her so she wouldn't have to be alone and a bedroom was offered to me, but I only kept my clothes there. Every night, Dana and I talked until we fell asleep. Sometimes I drifted off while she was still talking, or else I was the one talking when I realized she was no longer awake. Then I would think for a while until I too was sleeping.

One night that week it began to snow and didn't stop for two days. Three of Dana's performances were canceled, so she practiced in the front room of the house. In a different room I did my stretching. Afterward we went out into the snow, into the quiet. It had become a blanket, covering the city, covering something in me. It seemed to affect Dana too. She let go a bit of her seriousness. She was softer, looser in that weather.

I imagined her eating meat. Instead, she ate a bit of snow.

When we came inside, we changed out of our damp clothes and dressed comfortably for the evening. We made popcorn, and read, and sat in front of the parlor windows.

After I had read several chapters of the book I'd brought with me, I set it on my lap. The snow was again falling fast.

"I've never really been drunk," I said, "though once I shared half a drink with someone."

"Never? Even I have been."

"I want to be."

Dana set her book on the sofa. She disappeared from the parlor, then came back with two glasses of something sweet and strong. She handed one of the glasses to me and bowed.

Soon enough, I was walking anywhere in the house I wanted, sitting in every room; sometimes Dana was with me. Only once did I run into the maid, and she was the embarrassed one, even though I was the trespasser. Some of the time Dana and I were dancing; I'm sure the maid saw us then. A waltz, which made me think of Antoinette, then something much more frenzied than a waltz. I was happy when I was frenzied, when I was moving in that way. We danced until we had exhausted ourselves. I fell asleep on the sofa with Dana by my side.

Later I found myself alone again, at the enormous dining table. I didn't remember waking up. Against the far wall sat a huge cabinet filled with good china and copper candlesticks. How different houses were from each other, yet our cabinet was filled with the same things. But as much as it appeared static, the cabinet was a work in progress—what was in it would change. Some of the china would break. Perhaps some of it would be stolen. Later on we would all be dead, but the cabinet would remain, and the people who used it would be different, though likely related to the ones who had used it before.

"Here you are," Dana said, beside me again. "It's three in the morning. What are you thinking about?"

"Cabinets, dear Dana."

We went upstairs and undressed for bed, Dana helping me to unbutton the back of my dress, after which I helped her. Then I fell asleep feeling a little sick.

I DIDN'T WANT TO LEAVE, but one cannot stay away for too long, longer than is normal, even when one wishes to be abnormal, as my husband might say, and Dana's family was coming back. When I arrived at home the next evening, dinner was waiting, as I knew it would be. My husband and I ate together, me with a headache, a real one this time. There was our cabinet, the lights from the candles flickering upon it. I saw that ours was less beautiful than the other.

As I cut my food into little pieces, my husband watched me closely. He himself barely seemed to eat. "You look younger tonight," he said.

"We're both like children."

"I don't think so. Why do you say that?"

"Do you feel like an adult, truly?"

"Of course."

"Then I guess we are different in that way." I ate like a pig and paid attention to what my headache felt like. I had two things to focus on, my food and my pain. "Last night I got drunk. You'll have to forgive me, but I don't feel well."

My husband put down his spoon, not undramatically. "What was the occasion?"

"I wanted to."

"I see. Did you enjoy it?

"Yes. I liked that I was with Dana."

"Dana is lucky, then."

"No, I'm the lucky one."

My husband picked up his spoon again; then to my great surprise, I imagine because he was jealous, he said that we could smoke hashish.

"When?" was the only thing I managed to say. How indelicate.

We sat in the parlor and he showed me how to smoke, how to hold the little pipe, and how much to take in. There was a whole other world and he knew this world. I felt suddenly I didn't know him, yet I knew I never had. In another way, I was closer to him than I'd been before.

The hashish took away my headache and was pleasurable, more pleasurable than drinking. I thought I had known decadence, but this was something else entirely. I had not lain around in quite this way. I had not been this relaxed, and in my posture I was able to let down my guard. Everything my husband said I thought was funny. This was completely new.

We ate again and the food was delicious, the cider sweet and cold. Even the glass that held it, so clear.

Later, when the hashish had worn off, I went to our bedroom alone to lie down. From the bed, the bathroom door open, I could see the hook with my bathrobe hanging from it, my towel.

*There are my things*, I thought, with some astonishment and comfort. But what right did I have to a bathrobe like that, a towel? There are those who have neither, who must dry off with a pair of old pants. Even the quilt I was lying on was nicer than many of the clothes people got to wear, nicer than my own dresses had been, and something about that was obscene.

*Relax*, I told myself. *You don't have to think about this now. There is always tomorrow.*

I N THE MIDDLE OF WINTER I had gotten drunk and then high. I had spent time with my friend like this and then with my husband. If I'm honest, I enjoyed both. For a while such warmth was in my body, if not in the air, and I was able to carry these experiences with me.

In the parlor, my husband and I planned a trip to Brazil. I wanted to also go to a swamp.

"Why did you leave there?" I asked him.

"You're not the only one who's ever wanted to get away."

He was right; I paid little attention to what his life had been like, what it was now. But I didn't say that. I sat stiffly in my chair. Quite grotesque.

For Solange's birthday I got her a new dress, a pair of shoes, stockings, a bracelet, a long winter coat. As usual, she seemed to think it was odd, not only that I had given her presents, but so many of them. Still, she left the house that morning wearing all of it. She was to have a week off and I was happy for her. While she was gone, I cooked dinner twice, simple meals my husband didn't seem to care for, such as polenta or lentils, and the rest of the time we ate in restaurants.

Sometimes in the afternoons Dana came to visit after her rehearsals and we'd lie around in my study. We would talk about the ballet in which she was dancing. We would talk about my writing.

"Am I changing?" she asked dreamily.

"Yes, you're changing. But the best parts of you are still here."

She would kiss me on the cheek. She would pick up the books on my desk and look at them, the little objects I'd gathered on my walks. Then she was off. Her days were busy.

I, on the other hand, spent those days lost in my reading. I sat in front of the fire sometimes with my husband, and sometimes alone. I forgot where I was, so forceful were the settings and characters in those books I read, so fine and deep. Yet when I came to, it wasn't unpleasant. In fact, it pleased me very much.

THEN I BEGAN TO FEEL NERVOUS, and with that the pleasantness disappeared. I would wake up in the morning ready for something bad to happen. Again I felt that spring would never come, and the cold seemed dangerous. I thought of people freezing on the street. To have no home to go into would be horrible.

I felt the cold enter my writing, but I transformed it. Harsh, but not barren. I couldn't write like that. Dana practiced her dancing so often I was afraid she would break both her legs, and though I told her of my fear, she continued.

"It's the only thing I want to do," she said.

Writing was not the only thing I wanted to do, but the important thing, I thought, was that I wanted to do it more than anything else. I would write for an entire day, then do nothing for days on end. I'd look at my notebook and feel bored. After some time, however, it was my life that was boring, and I missed writing, so I would begin to write again.

I went on like that, writing, not writing, carrying

something anxious with me, waking up in the night or the morning with a sense of dread.

It was hard to eat; I didn't want food. But I would force myself to eat it, even if it took me a long time. Solange would come to the table when I was eating lunch or breakfast, confused I was still there.

"Do you not like your lunch, madame?"

"I like it, but I don't have an appetite right now."

"Shall I clear it from the table?"

"No, I want to try."

And so I would.

At dinner my husband was impatient. When things became difficult for me, my husband made them worse. Even reading offered no escape, the suffering of the characters was so great:

*"But tired as I was, I couldn't sleep. I thought of Alice, and then of Rufus, and I realized that Rufus had done exactly what I had said he would do: gotten possession of the woman without having to bother with her husband. Now, somehow, Alice would have to accept not only the loss of her husband, but her own enslavement. Rufus had caused her trouble, and now he had been rewarded for it. It made no sense."*

T O BE ALIVE *and sometimes grieving. To eat dinners and sit in restaurants. To sleep with my husband and then tell Solange which rooms need cleaning. To clean my own study and then read in it. To sit in a dark theater with a lit stage in front of me. To walk with Antoinette and then with Dana. Walking along the lake, the snow falling on my boots, my hat.*

*There are the waves that rise differently in the cold temperature, the animals lifting their heads. If I lift my head too? Dana lifting her head onstage.*

*The cold air sets high above the buildings and I go downstairs. To my husband, our life together.*

*If the fascination can move inside, is it not also within*

*me? And at the same time outside with the leaves, which are blowing along the street? Outside with the stray dogs, who have all of their freedom but not enough comfort. We were born to die, but death can feel unreal if we're comforted in the right ways. And if we cannot comfort ourselves, are there other tricks to keep it distant? Death will come no matter how comfortable we are; it doesn't work in that way even if we feel it might. Today, for instance, I am far from it. But on other days: will it happen* here, here, *or* here*? I imagine it while crossing the street. On those days I am much too close.*

*The women working in the glue factory, I think of them often. Why was I saved from that life, from a mass of dead horses? We should memorialize the horses, remember them truthfully, and the women who have to spend their days in that way. Yet I too have used glue. I have benefited from a woman who never stops working, walking back from the factory in the morning and the night.*

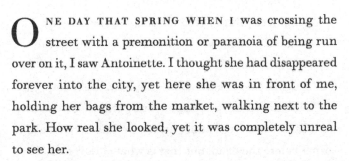

O NE DAY THAT SPRING WHEN I was crossing the
street with a premonition or paranoia of being run
over on it, I saw Antoinette. I thought she had disappeared
forever into the city, yet here she was in front of me,
holding her bags from the market, walking next to the
park. How real she looked, yet it was completely unreal
to see her.

"Antoinette," I called, and when she turned around, I
asked, "Are you alive?"

"What a question. Of course I am. I could ask you the
same."

I must have been as unreal to her indeed, appearing
as if from thin air after having been gone for so long.

I couldn't help studying her, with her long brown hair braided becomingly around her head. She wore a dull dress, but it was gathered at the waist with a colorful sash, and that made it pleasing.

As I looked at her, she looked at me also.

"You're different from when I last saw you," she said.

"I married someone rich. Is that what you mean?"

She nodded. "It agrees with you."

"I'm still trying to figure out myself whether it does or not." I smiled. I couldn't help myself. I was nearly ecstatic. "You're different too. It's been two years."

"I suppose I am. Lots of things have happened."

"Like what? Tell me."

"I got married too, for one thing."

"Antoinette, I'm so glad for you. Do you love him?"

"Endlessly. He's a very kind man. And handsome."

"And is he poor?"

"Yes, but I don't care about that now. We're happy."

While we spoke, a group of young children stood near us, a little too close, I thought, for we had arrived at the corner before they had, but that is what children do. They had come from the zoo, and their teacher was giving them a lesson on the animals they'd just seen.

"The one-humped camel is from the Middle East and the Horn of Africa," she said in a high voice.

"And the two-humped camel?" a child yelled out. Another child started crying.

"And you, do you love your husband?" Antoinette asked, in the midst of all this.

"I like him very much. And admire him greatly."

"I see."

Whether I loved my husband was of no interest; I wanted to change the subject. "Antoinette, I'm very sorry I never said goodbye. It was wrong of me not to tell you I was going away." Though I sounded almost completely phony when I said this, it was not how I felt. The emotion was intensely true, but I wasn't able to communicate it in the way I was experiencing it.

"Don't be silly, you have nothing to apologize for."

I took her hand. Next to us the child was crying still. "Nothing? What do you mean? What kind of friend does that?"

"I assume you did what you needed, that you had your reasons." She glanced at the teacher, who had moved to comfort the child, then went on, "But it's true I was hurt then. You were there with me at the museum, and then one day you were gone. At first I was worried, but one of the others said she saw you in a shop, looking quite fine."

"Yes, I was okay."

"Well, it doesn't matter now, that's what I mean. I've moved on. It's nothing you should dwell on."

"Will you visit me? Please? I want to know you again. Will you do it soon?" I tore a page out of my notebook and wrote down my address, and though I wasn't sure she would actually come, she promised me she would.

The city streets alive with daily life, I walked through them marveling that finally I had seen her. It had taken so long, yet it happened. I hoped we could be friends again. Even seeing her for those few moments had brought a great warmth.

At home I lay in bed, thinking, and when my husband came to the bedroom, I told him what had happened, but I felt he took it lightly. "I thought she would be angry at me, and she admitted she had been hurt, but it seems she's forgiven me already."

"Isn't that a good thing?" My husband touched my face awkwardly for a moment, but he didn't stay with me. Soon, I heard his footsteps moving down the hall. I heard Solange there too, the great soother.

Then I was alone and I didn't like it. *Maybe I should be alone always*, I thought.

That night I read through dinner. I didn't join my husband in front of the fire.

He ignored that absence, but he didn't ignore me when he came to bed. "Are you unhappy again?" he asked me.

"I'm pensive, but I guess you wouldn't understand something like that."

"Wouldn't I? What is it I'd understand, then?"

"Card games and work."

"Is that all?"

"I don't know. You tell me."

"You're quite mean when you want to be." He turned away toward the wall and I turned toward the other, the very picture of an unhappy couple, an unhappy marriage. We were not long for this world.

It was true, I was mean sometimes. But I didn't have it in me to be kind to someone who saw me only in relation to property and propriety. To be domestic first and then to be a shallow vessel out and about in the world. Didn't he understand that was not who I was? I wondered why he had chosen me. And why had I chosen him? Had it been for survival, for experience? Both of those things, I guess.

I T TOOK ANTOINETTe so long to visit I gave up on the idea, but one miraculously warm, rainy morning there was she was at the front door. While she took off her muddy boots and arranged her hair in the hall mirror, I watched her closely. I was happy to see her.

"You're soaking wet. I'll find you some dry clothes."

"I'll be okay."

"You can't sit down like that. You'll be uncomfortable."

"I won't."

But I insisted and went upstairs to get one of my favorite dresses. Beautiful, but not excessive. White and black, two colors I loved together. I knew she would look lovely in it. In the parlor, she sat in front of the windows with green trees behind her.

"You're a vision," I said. "I want you to keep it."

"I couldn't. It's yours, Vitória."

"But it looks so much nicer on you than it does me."

"I'm sure it doesn't."

"I'm certain it does."

A pitcher of lemonade was on the table next to us, and after our initial insistence and resistance I poured us each a glass of it. I offered her a slice of blueberry pie.

"Tell me more about your life," I said. "I want to know what it's like now."

"I'm going to have a baby." She smiled. "I'm almost twelve weeks pregnant."

"That's wonderful, Antoinette. You'll have the most adorable baby, I'm sure of it. Are you happy?"

"I don't think I've ever been more at peace." She blushed and ate a forkful of pie. "I've not always been happy, you know." She looked at me warmly. "And you, will you and your husband have a child soon?"

"No." I laughed. "I don't think I was meant to."

"What do you mean?"

"I mean I haven't yet wanted to be a mother." I took a sip of my lemonade. "And I haven't become pregnant even though my husband and I have made love many times."

"I'm not surprised."

"Why, can you tell by looking at me?"

"Of course not. But it fits what I remember of you." She paused. "Outside of the things you wanted, you always told me what you didn't want too."

I didn't yet know what I could say to Antoinette, how candid I could be. Our renewed friendship was only at its beginning. Who knew if it would go on.

"Do you enjoy sex with your husband?" I asked.

"Yes. Do you enjoy sex with yours?"

"It's the part of my marriage I enjoy most of all."

"I suppose that's all right. At least there's something you enjoy about it."

"That's true. After I have an orgasm I feel healthy. Like having a perfect night's sleep, or walking across the city, or swimming. And I almost feel close to my husband. Not quite, but almost."

"I feel infinitely close to Frederick then."

As Antoinette and I went on, I found myself at peace too. I was still surprised she wasn't angry or upset with me; I didn't understand it, but I let it go. I was just happy to know her again.

We didn't see each other as often as I saw Dana, but when she could get away, she visited me, or we took walks as we had those years before. I wanted to visit her, but at first she wouldn't allow it. She said she was too embarrassed for me to see where she lived.

"But why? I haven't always lived in a house like the one I'm living in now, you know that. And who knows if I always will?"

S OON IT WAS SUMMER and I was again filled with longing and glad for that longing. The lake, calm and alive, growing darker as the day grew dark, gaining movement as the fronds of those date trees had, showing me something of life, how to exist.

I would let myself get hot before swimming into the water. I did this all day, hot and then cold. How lucky I was. The other people on the beach unpacking their lunches, the children burying one another in the sand and then breaking free, chasing one another.

I knew then that I could write however I wanted, that I need not shy away, even if I must shy away in conversation with people I didn't love. The gentle waves washing over the sand, sex, friendship, the ballet, the desert, the tropics, the paintings, they had helped me.

I began to write with more energy and focus, and I read when I got tired. I walked from one side of the city to the other and back again.

Soon, Antoinette started to show even more . . .

One morning, when it was already warm, Dana and I

sat in the park. I tried to read from the book I had brought with me, but I couldn't because Dana was reading my notebook. No one had ever read my writing before, so I was alert and nervous and distracted.

"You mustn't watch me. I won't be able to focus."

"I'm sorry, but I'm afraid."

"Don't be afraid. Look, if you're going to watch, you should let me take the notebook home so I can read it in peace."

"I can't be without it."

"Then do something else."

I read my book as long as my attention would allow me, then I began to write in that book too, though I had never written in any book before. I tried to keep my books as perfect as I could, but this was the only thing that would stop me from looking at Dana.

After some time had passed, Dana turned to me. "You write so nicely of the paintings, Vitória, so evocatively. I feel I am standing in front of them, and that you are there too, showing them to me. What a guide you are, a spiritual guide almost, one I wouldn't have imagined."

How happy I was. I had created an experience for someone; I hadn't been sure I could actually do that.

From then on, Dana asked to read from my notebook from time to time and then she would talk with me about what she'd read. "A humble sense of purpose," she said once, "and of fascination. You are fascinated by everything around you." On a few occasions I did let her take my notebook home, when I thought I wouldn't need it, that it might be good for me to be without it for a while. If I found I wanted to write, I opened up the same book I had written in already and wrote there again. I had already defaced it, and I was starting to feel as if I were having a conversation with it.

TODAY AT THE MUSEUM, *looking at paintings of the night. How serene they are. Without trying, you can almost absorb their quiet. First I stood in front of mountains I've never stood before in person, maybe never will. Yet they didn't seem far. Granite peaks and a green meadow spread out below.*

*Then other paintings of other nights, in England the sky the most satisfying shade of black. A strange Arizona, with an emerald-green sky, a pale green moon, the mountains a metallic color.*

*Then I looked at the most curious one of all, less serene than the ones before it. The wind is heavy, the trees in the distance blowing sideways, and a lady is all in white, her shawl swept up over her head. Is it her maid who is accompanying her? It looks like it. Are they hurrying together to another place, escaping something we are unable to see? Maybe that is why the maid has turned around; she is making sure they are safe. And in this painting there the two remain.*

"You're different now," my husband remarked, and

he liked me again, now that I wasn't having trouble. We were sitting in the garden together; it was late for us to be out there, but our own night was still immensely pleasant, with its warm air and dark leaves and grass, the bright house behind us. It didn't make sense to be inside.

"Different in what way?"

"You know what I mean. From how you've been."

From the bushes the cat emerged and jumped onto my lap and the dog barked at her sudden appearance. I stroked behind her ears, under her chin. She was so soft. I was not, and that was part of the problem.

"It's not that I've changed."

My husband said nothing in return.

I sighed, for I knew I was giving him hardly anything. "It's true I'm doing better now. The summer makes me happy," I tried.

This should have been a reconciliation, and he did take my hand, but instead I was restless. I wanted to write more than I wanted to sit next to him; I enjoyed looking at paintings more than his conversation. I didn't even want to have sex, and that was something new.

W HEN MY HUSBAND WORKED LATE, I had Dana over for dinner, and once in a while Antoinette, when she could get away, when her husband was working late too. I wanted to help fatten her up for her pregnancy. Or I ate alone; I would daydream by candlelight in front of the dishes that sat quietly on the table. Sometimes I brought my notebook with me, writing in it just a sentence or two. A leaf falling from a tree, I could see it from where I sat. Now someone would step on it, probably my husband.

What was it I wanted then? If I think back?

Well, there were too many things.

I didn't want to be invisible, though sometimes I treated others as though they themselves were. My notebook in my hands changing the energy in the room. All of us do this, change the rooms we're in.

Picturing the river, empty of people. Some things are better left that way. Picturing that void on the lake.

Picturing Dana putting on her costume, walking up the stairs to the stage. In which moment is she most herself? She is unfolding, always. Antoinette too. I would picture her at home, not knowing what her house looked like.

I would see these things so clearly and then eat my stew. For the first time, I had asked Solange not to put meat in it.

"But you'll want meat for your other meals, I assume?"

"No, I'm tired of it."

I thought that was that, yet she continued to put meat in everything, not every night, but when I was eating alone. That meant something, I'm sure of it. She was trying to play games with me. She would say she had forgotten, but everything else she did perfectly, especially for my husband.

"Solange," I would say in frustration, "you've given me meat again."

"I'm so sorry, madame."

"Take it away. I'm done with it."

"Of course."

"Please bring me the basket of biscuits."

I had quite a few biscuits during that time.

S OLANGE HATES ME," I whined to Antoinette, the stage in front of us empty and bright, waiting for the dancers, for movement. I had brought Antoinette with me to the ballet; it was her first time, as mine had been not so long ago.

"I'm sure she doesn't. What on earth for?"

"She's cold for no reason. She always has been, and when I tell her I don't want meat in my meals, she gives it to me anyway. She ignores everything I say."

"She probably can't remember. It's so unusual, after all. Everyone eats meat."

"Sometimes I see her looking at my husband, studying him. I wouldn't doubt that she's in love with him. Or maybe she's trying to figure something out, but what that could be, I don't know."

Antoinette took my hand, and we stayed like that as the music began and the curtain rose to the ceiling.

The dancers were animated in a different way that night; their movements seemed to begin from a different place, which I was enthralled by. But I was always enthralled; I knew this about myself. It was almost annoying. As usual, some energy was in Dana that surrounded only her, but she danced in perfect synchronicity all the same, the dancers leaping across the stage almost as one being, then breaking apart, becoming their own selves. I enjoyed this coming together, this breaking apart. I wanted to do it in my writing.

"Which one is Dana?" Antoinette whispered.

"There to the right, at the very end." There she was, dressed in bright red like a rare flower.

"She dances like a dream."

"I know, doesn't she?"

Dana, not warm or cold, just endlessly present.

In the second act, the dancers wore long dresses and greeted each other as if they were at a ball. They broke into pairs, and the stage was much darker than it had been before. I felt a strange anticipation. In that scene it was night and candles were in the windows of the room they danced in. Before this, they had been outside. In their pairs, they danced closely for a long time, then when they were tired, they rested on the floor. Something about watching them lie there like that was relaxing. It made me want to slide down in my seat too.

D RAWINGS OF WITCHES *and old women; they float in the air and grab on to one another's clothing. A braid of women, a clump.*

*In one drawing, four figures are floating: two pairs ascending or falling, we don't know which. The two in the foreground are barely holding on; an old woman is laughing gleefully while pulling another woman's hair, that second woman crying out in pain. It must be pain. If they are falling, she will be the first to hit the ground. The second pair touch the first and they look as if they are embracing. They are shadows, drawn all in gray.*

*The clumping, what does it mean? Are they intimate or is it more abject than that?*

*In another drawing, a group of people are clumped together in a tree. The drawing is still but it seems as though the people are fidgeting. They look like children in that way. But somehow the drawing is somber, as if everyone is sick.*

*The caption below the drawing reads, "In this print, a group of figures has settled on the branch of a tree. Some have been identified as witches and others as members of the nobility. They are being lectured, but not all are paying attention."*

*I can't tell who is a witch and who is a noble. The clump, that's all I see.*

O NE DAY WHILE AT THE LIBRARY, I found out there was to be a reading the following week by an author I liked. How exciting, I thought. After reading from his novel, the author would be interviewed by another author. Questions would be taken from the audience. I had never been to a reading before.

The evening of the event I dressed carefully. I wore gold earrings, a full, dark-colored skirt, and a light-colored blouse. I wanted to be simple and elegant. Not that anyone would be watching. I hoped I looked like a writer. I did feel like one.

I walked to the reading, and when I looked at the streets, I saw a city filled with people I didn't know, would probably never know. It didn't bother me; it's the same for everyone. When people look at me, they also see a stranger. In a way it is good, and I smiled at the thought of being a stranger walking down the street.

At the reading, the author spoke in a loud voice that was also dramatic, yet he wasn't reading a dramatic part. Every so often, he looked at the audience with a great amount of purpose. It was difficult to want to look back. The few times he looked at me, I looked immediately past him, to the window with the night sky in it. At least I had something else on which to focus my attention, something open and calm. Or I looked at the wastebasket, completely still. I didn't like him, and I hadn't expected that. I didn't like the man who interviewed him either, who spoke out of turn, I thought, of his own success, both at the start of the interview and then again sometime in the middle of their conversation.

That second author said, "When you are first given accolades for your work, it is tremendously exciting, but it soon becomes tiresome." I didn't believe him. If it were true, why would he be saying it now? It meant something to him to be able to say it. He probably hadn't been able to stop himself, as I sometimes had trouble not saying something I later regretted. Or maybe he would never regret it, thought it important to the conversation he and the author were having.

I wanted to lock them in the room after the reading was over and make them listen to each other forever. Let them look at the sky when they got tired, or the wastebasket. I thought they deserved that. I wanted to tell them how terrible the reading had been, that it had ruined the writing, how shallow the interview, how much I had hated all of it.

When I walked out of the room, I said simply, "You're

both worms," and they looked at me, not knowing how to respond to a statement like that. "Of the worst kind. When you open your mouths, you are male worms eating from a toilet."

THE NEXT MORNING AT BREAKFAST I tried to tell Solange what I was writing. I'd never bothered before and I don't know what made me try. I wanted to communicate something, I guess. I wanted to say something about myself, about how I spent my days. I was trying a final time, perhaps, to connect. It didn't go well.

"I'm writing about myself looking at paintings," I told her. "And sometimes at plants."

"Is there an audience for that?"

"I'm sure there is not."

"What makes you do it, then?"

"My soul," I said boldly. I didn't care how it sounded. I ate my oatmeal. It wasn't something in which Solange could put meat.

Solange had no reply; she was so involved in washing my husband's dishes from breakfast you wouldn't think I had said anything at all. She folded a dish towel neatly, then folded a dishrag. I had never before seen a person fold a wet dishrag.

"It's too wet to fold it now, Solange. It'll never dry that way."

"How would you know anything about dishrags?"

It was so direct I didn't know how to respond. If I said, "I have used a dishrag my entire life, up until these last two years," and said it with too much feeling, I would sound ridiculous. I knew that and I said it anyway. My voice was dramatic.

Solange unfolded the rag and laid it on the table next to where I was eating, which was the most ridiculous thing of all.

"As you wish, madame. Here is your rag."

"I'm going out," I said angrily, and I took my rain jacket and went.

As was common for me, I instantly started walking in the direction of the museum. My notebook in my jacket pocket; maybe that was a kind of clumping, what I tried to pull close. I put my hand in my pocket several times to make sure my notebook was still there. *Solange is a witch*, I thought, *and I hate her. I am a witch too. Neither of us is noble.*

In one of the galleries was a small collection of unfinished works I hadn't yet looked at, and I went to them before anything else. Paintings with empty space in them, I thought I should see that. They hung as confidently as any other painting would, unfinished or not, several on each wall.

In this one, blank faces and faces undone. In this one, a dog not yet filled in. In this one, a landscape missing. A brightly lit woman on top of darkness. This last one sent me back to Solange, which bothered me to no end.

I found a table in a corridor and sat down to write. I thought this would help. In the museum, even a corridor was beautiful, with its intricate molding and views of the galleries, and the table was elegant and fine. I had never sat at it when I worked here, but I had cleaned it all the same. Now I sat here often.

*Why is empty space a comfort and a relief? It's not because I project myself there; it's because I can't. It shows me my projections, but they haven't left my mind. Empty space remains empty, always. And for a little while a small part of me can be empty too.*

When I went outside, it was drizzling again and the air was humid. Paintings and the air, so much better than Solange and me, and I found myself a bit restored. Solange and I would never be friends; maybe we would only be enemies.

I T TOOK A WHILE, but finally Antoinette gave me permission to come to her house. It wasn't as run-down as she had told me, but it was small, fit for one person. She and her husband lived in one room.

"What will you do when you have the baby?"

"We will live here still," she said cheerfully. "And in a few years I hope we can move."

Antoinette had made it pleasant, or maybe she and her husband had made it pleasant together. I never knew how people did things. It was crowded, her sofa and chairs were plain, but she had found an oval rug, not fancy, but pretty all the same. Her and Frederick's room was cozy, and the happiness they shared there was easy to imagine.

I arrived at four o'clock and we sat through the afternoon. At one point, it hailed. I took that as a good sign, something momentous in the air. At first it had surprised us, as hail always will, the balls of ice knocking against the windows. We opened the door and watched them hit the ground, melting almost instantly.

At seven o'clock, Antoinette's husband came home, carrying a loaf of bread. Antoinette had already made the soup. She'd made it without meat so I could eat with them.

"I'm Vitória." I didn't offer my hand. I didn't want things to be formal.

"Frederick," he said. "It's good to meet you."

His clothes were old and worn, it was true, but I couldn't take my eyes off him, and him with Antoinette. I was drawn to their warmth. In that way he looked better than my husband.

The three of us ate our soup and bread and talked easily, about our childhoods and our families, where we had lived. We ate the peach pie I had brought, I washed the dishes, and when I walked home, they walked with me, Frederick pointing out the stars and the constellations. I had had a good time that night.

"There," he said. "Do you see the Big Dipper?"

We stopped to take it in, burning its shape gently into the dark sky. We weren't different from the cucumber, the melon, the lettuce, the apple. Not really.

"If I move to the country," I said, "will you visit me there?"

"Of course, but that would be silly," Antoinette said. "Where would you live?"

"In a one-room house."

"But Frederick and I live in a one-room house," Antoinette responded.

The darkness was behind her again, as it had been in the museum when we had first become friends. Only this time it was soothing.

F INALLY IT WAS AUTUMN AGAIN, and Antoinette had her baby. I went over to their room when I could to help clean and cook, to keep Antoinette company in the afternoons. But it wasn't just that. They kept me company too.

She wasn't as peaceful as she had been in the months previous, afraid she would do something wrong, and it was hard for her not to sleep. Both she and Frederick looked a little haggard, not that I would have told them that. I'm sure I sometimes looked haggard too, and I had no baby to keep me awake. We cycle in and out of different ways of being, of appearing in the world.

"I want to baptize little Frederick," Antoinette told me one day. We were walking along the street, the baby in his carriage. "We'll do it at the church Frederick's family attends."

"Why? I didn't even know you were religious."

"I was baptized, and so was Frederick. It's tradition."

"But little Frederick won't know what's happening. It won't mean anything to him."

"It doesn't matter. We'll know what's happening and it will mean something to us. He'll be able to sense that."

"Not all traditions are worth following, you know." Antoinette didn't respond, so I went on. "I just don't like seeing a baby in the water in that way, religiously, especially because they have no choice in the matter. I was baptized too and I watched my brothers and sisters when their turns came around. I always felt strange. Shouldn't we be able to decide for ourselves?"

"What does it matter to you if we follow tradition? Frederick isn't your baby, Vitória, he's ours."

"I didn't say he was."

"Then you shouldn't worry. The baby will not necessarily be like you, or believe in the same things. And maybe he won't be like us, but he'll be baptized as we were."

I looked at little Frederick. He was sucking on two of his fingers. Intensely, he resembled Antoinette. "You're right. It's none of my business."

Antoinette touched my shoulder gently. "I don't mind if you don't like baptisms, but you shouldn't mind if I do."

"Yes, I'm sorry." I meant it.

Little Frederick tried to grab one of his feet. He wanted to put it in his mouth too.

We are such oral creatures, especially at that age, trying to learn about the world. Antoinette bent to button his jacket, then she buttoned her own. Tradition or not, she was a good mother. I could see that.

Little Frederick would be baptized the next month. I would attend the baptism because Antoinette was my friend.

I DON'T HAVE SEX NOW, though once at a farmhouse it did happen. Believe it or not, I was invited to a farmhouse party and I went, though I found no one like Dana or Antoinette, or even Solange. It was surprising how easy it was to have sex again, so I don't think it is gone from me forever. There will be another party, or there will be another person in my life. Lately I've had a vision of drinking a glass of water while lying in a bath. Or a grouping of vegetables on a counter meant for preparing a vegetable soup. I think about the things we need to live. Not my jewelry, which I have laid out similarly on a table in the hallway, which I sometimes still wear, one at a time.

In every painting, someone or something emerges. I emerged here into the country. I emerged walking along these dull streets, close to my own mind and what I know of life. Close to my blind spots, my limitations as a person, the limits of what I can perceive, at least for now. I am deeply flawed.

The important thing is that I not harden, that I keep something open in myself, that I remember what it's like to emerge at fourteen, twenty, and on and on. In some ways unchanged, but in other ways so different. That I not harden into "Vitória in the country" and all that entails for me.

I won't stay here forever, but I told myself I would give it a year. A year to focus myself completely, a year without distractions. I miss my friends. I'll want to see them again.

T HE MORNING OF THE BAPTISM, Antoinette and
Frederick were radiant; it was a public welcoming
to little Frederick, after all, not just to the church. Wel-
come to the world!

I met Antoinette's brother and sister, who now lived
with their aunt, but not her mother, for she had finally
died too. I met Frederick's parents, who were kind and
cheerful. They invited me to sit next to them and I did. I
hadn't been in a church for a long time.

It wasn't the kind of baptism I had pictured, little
Frederick being pushed down in the water, Antoinette
and Frederick and the minister standing in the water
too. Instead, the minister sprinkled him with water three

times at the front of the church. I was disturbed, but I hoped I conveyed seriousness instead. It would have been wrong to show any part of what I felt, so I tried my best to keep a mild expression on my face, but who knows what that actually looked like. Antoinette held little Frederick in her arms and he cried when the water was sprinkled on his body. He cried often, as babies do; it wasn't symbolic. He had been crying even before the ceremony began.

Afterward we ate a plain cake in the basement of the church and I embraced the happy family, all of the somber feeling of a baptism now gone. The churchgoers took turns holding little Frederick, gazing at him, and talking as one does to a baby. Sometimes their voices surprised me. You never know what a person's baby voice will sound like, or his or her pet voice. I talked to the dog and the cat in a high voice, for instance.

When I felt it was safe to leave, that I had been present for a proper amount of time, I said my goodbyes. I could hardly wait to get out of there. Outside, the sky looked like a cliché of heaven, with its big fluffy white clouds, or maybe being inside the church too long had made it appear that way, connected to churchgoing in some way.

When I got home, my husband was sitting in the den reading his paper, taking up his pipe, as men sometimes do. In another life, it might have been comforting to see him there, to return home to someone I loved.

"How was it?" He took a puff.

"Okay, I guess. If you like baptisms."

"Well, I suppose we're next."

I made some kind of strange sound as I went gloomily up the stairs. I don't know if he heard me. I don't think I cared.

MEANWHILE, Dana was becoming a bit famous. When I was on the street with her, or in a café or a shop, sometimes people noticed. They had seen her onstage and were now seeing her on the sidewalk. The way she walked was different from what it had been when we first met; it couldn't be helped. When you hold yourself so consciously all of the time, I don't think it goes away. She was surprised by the attention, sometimes made uncomfortable by it, but at some moments she seemed to like it too. Maybe because of it, she rarely talked about dance anymore. She kept that for herself. She seemed centered, more centered than I could ever hope to be.

"I'm afraid," I told her in my uncentered way. We were sitting in a café, and sure enough, it seemed the woman at the next table would approach us at any moment. She had furtively glanced several times at Dana. "My husband brought up the idea of a baby."

"Vitória, you've been married now for almost three years. He's bound to think of it sooner or later, don't you agree?"

"I guess, but why is it necessary for everyone to think of it, as if there were no other choice? His standing probably somehow demands it. He is required to be a father."

"Or perhaps he truly wants it, as people often do." I failed to return the conversation back to her, and she went on, "Why do you think it hasn't happened?"

"I don't know, but sometimes I feel I have willed it. In reality, there must be something wrong with one of us. Or both. I hope that's the case."

"I hope there's nothing wrong with you. But I also hope you don't become pregnant, not if you don't want to be."

"Thank you."

"And how is Antoinette's baby?"

"He's sweet. Just like his mother and father. When I see them all together, it makes such sense. He reaches for things already. If I'm eating something, he tries to get it. But he doesn't cry if he can't have it. He's just curious."

"They want everything they can get their hands on."

"And their mouths."

Dana bent her head to drink her coffee and the woman next to us got up from her seat and seemed to head toward us, but I gave her a cold stare. That sent her in the other direction and I was proud of that moment. I had never before sent someone away in that manner.

A FEW MONTHS AFTER little Frederick was born, Antoinette settled into her routine, playing with him in the mornings, and in the afternoons while he slept, she began to make clothes. She had made them for her family when she was younger, but had put sewing aside for a while. It didn't take long for her to find her way again. She was much more patient and careful than she had been before. She lost that sense of doing nothing she'd had at the museum, and soon something in how she dressed was exciting, such as a red wool sweater dress that rose high on the neck, was fitted on top, then flowed fully from the waist, falling midway down the leg. When women looked at her on the street, I could tell they took notice, especially when she was wearing this dress; still, they never paid her a compliment. Women can be horrible in that way. I complimented her repeatedly.

She also made things for her husband and baby, and for my birthday she made me a long pleated skirt that fit perfectly. She didn't think I would wear it. The material wasn't fancy enough, she said, but I assured her I didn't need fancy cloth.

When Dana saw the skirt, she wanted Antoinette to make something for her too. Now Antoinette's designs were finally receiving their compliments. Someone known and admired was wearing them.

Though I had expected her to after the baptism, Antoinette rarely went to church on Sundays. Still, on Wednesday evenings she went to mass to sing hymns and listen to the choir. "Will you come with me?" she asked. "Just once. I know you're not religious, but you don't have to be. They sing so beautifully, Vitória, as if they really were angels. You would love it, I know you would."

So one Wednesday I went with her to St. Sophia's, a narrow cathedral lit by what must have been a hundred candles. The parish sat on one side, the choir on the other, facing each other. At the front of the chapel hung a painting of Christ. I'll admit that the room pleased me. Its narrowness, the long, tapered candles, the raised pews, which were unusually steep, all gave the sense that the room was more vertical than horizontal. I guessed the point was that the believers were already ascending to heaven when they worshipped and sang here, that they were in proximity to God. Though I didn't feel close to God, I enjoyed that sensation.

When the choir began to sing, they were truly angelic,

exulted in the candlelight. In our pew, Antoinette and I sat upright and received the voices. The narrow benches did not allow for slumping. That it was night changed something. I had always hated daytime in a church, heavy and overdramatic in the sunlight, as the baptism had been. One should only be in a church when it is dark outside.

As I listened to the choir, I found myself thinking about my husband; I didn't know what I should do. I didn't want to have sex with him anymore, nor did I want to have a child. How could I stay married to him? I didn't want to go back to having no money either, to cleaning the museum, but I couldn't stay where I was forever. I had no vision of it; it didn't seem true.

Solange came to my mind. Though I had never seen him look at her with anything more than the eyes of an employer, there were those times I'd seen her look at him. Didn't he deserve someone who would gaze at him in a way I never did? Did she love him?

I came back to the voices all around. Now even Antoinette was singing, and I opened the hymnal in front of me and sang for a while too. I knew these songs; I had sung them when I was a child. But soon enough it all fell away again in my attention and I returned to my marriage. I suppose I was meant for all I had experienced: the writing, the dance classes, my friendship with Dana, the places to which I had traveled, even my relationship.

I was grateful for it, but it was time to move on. If I left my husband, I would have to work again, yes. But if he had a reason to leave me? Then he might feel compelled to support me. Could I make him do that?

Antoinette shook me gently. "Vitória, the service is over." She was already gathering her things.

"I'm sorry. My mind was racing a hundred miles a minute. I couldn't keep it still."

"What were you thinking about?"

"My poor husband."

"Why poor?"

"Because I don't want him. I don't want to be married anymore."

"I figured that was coming."

"But I want him to leave me, not the other way around."

"Do you think he's been faithful?"

"I'm not sure. With any luck, he hasn't."

T HE NEXT TIME I SAW DANA, I complained about my husband to her too. I saw that I might become insufferable, that I might have to do a lot of complaining from here on out.

"In novels," I said, "men have affairs with their maids. If only I could encourage him somehow without him knowing that's what I'm doing."

I thought Dana would disapprove, but she didn't. "Or Solange," she answered.

"I've thought of that, actually. I'm not sure who would be harder to convince."

"You've said something seems funny with her when it comes to him. Maybe she just needs a little push. Permission from you."

Could my husband pass from me to Solange? Or was that idea too good to be true? She seemed so alone, yet it didn't have to be that way. I had gotten married, after all, and to a rich man, which I had never foreseen. Life changes and veers and becomes something new.

Now when I saw Solange in the house, I carried this

thought with me, and though in any other situation it would have added an extra layer of awkwardness and tension, the relationship between us was already so awkward and tense, it didn't seem to change anything at all. It gave me room to consider it, to work up to talking to her. But just when I thought I would, I lost my nerve.

*Speak to her,* I told myself. *Try to gauge the waters.* No conversation I had ever had with her had gone well, yet maybe this one would. It had to do with her future, after all.

I didn't think breakfast or even lunch the proper time to bring it up—every time I had tried it during those hours I had almost instantly failed—so I waited until one of the evenings when my husband was working late. I felt it should be dark outside, that in a certain sense everything should be at rest. That Solange should have let down her guard in some way. That I should have let down my guard too.

What a strange thing to bring up, to bring into being. If I failed at this conversation, all would be lost.

It was after dinner and Solange had not brought me meat, having finally given that up. I was sitting in the living room, a book in my hand, in tune, I thought, with reality.

It was now or never. I called her name when she walked near the room.

"Yes, madame."

I felt the weirdest I ever had and was momentarily hesitant, yet I went ahead with it. I had to.

"Solange, I apologize in advance, but I'm afraid I have to be blunt about something."

"Dinner?"

"No, it was fine. There's something else I want to talk to you about."

"All right, then."

"I've thought I've seen you, well . . . look at my husband sometimes. Is that right?"

"Look at him in what way?" She was already offended.

"With love, maybe."

"With love, madame? I look at him for my directions, that's the only way I look."

"I should say right off that it's okay if you look at him like that."

Solange was astonished, or at least she appeared that way, but we can never know what's in someone's mind. Anyway, she stared at me with some disbelief.

"I have no idea what you mean."

"Don't you?"

"You'll have to enlighten me."

"Solange, it means that I don't love my husband, and I think it's possible that you do. Or at least like him. Or you might enjoy another kind of life. I would like to leave this house, but I don't know how."

"Then you should figure it out on your own."

"That's the thing, I think I have. But it involves you, unfortunately. I had this idea, forgive me if it was a stupid one, that you might want him. If it's true, I think we could figure out a way for you to have him."

"I've never liked you, madame, but truly I had no idea just how much."

"But don't you see, your decision doesn't have to have anything to do with me. Solange, what do you want your life to be like? Would this help you get it?"

She tried to leave then and I called her back. I couldn't give up without even a small fight.

"I won't apologize for speaking to you in this way," she said. "Not after what you've said to me."

"I don't want you to apologize. I want you to help me, and help yourself in the process. If that's possible."

She stormed out and no amount of calling her back would do. Well, it was a warm-up, at least. I had broached the topic. She knew what was in my mind and heart. I didn't know what was in hers.

F OR THREE WEEKS, I failed to bring it up again, and Solange and I were more at odds around each other than we'd ever been; we had finally crossed a line. I had crossed it. If my husband noticed, he didn't say anything. He came and went, and when he was at home, he left me alone more than he usually did. I had rejected his advances several times, and that seemed to change something in him. When he was gone, Solange expressed herself angrily. She slammed cupboard doors, put plates and saucers down roughly on the counters. I felt she might break them, and then I began to see that it wouldn't work, that I had affected her quite negatively. I wasn't ready to give up, but the feeling in the house was becoming unbearable. I would obviously have to let it go. If I could.

"Solange," I said one day, "I'm sorry for——"

She left the room; she wouldn't allow me to say anything. That night she served me steak for dinner and I didn't dare ask for anything else. Instead, I took a break from eating. The next night she served it again, the same one, I believe, from the night before. From then on I started eating dinner out. We couldn't do this forever.

Then something incredible happened, if such a thing can be considered incredible. It was incredible for me.

One morning I told my husband I would be going to a play that evening, and I did go, but halfway through the performance I began to feel nauseous and left during intermission. When I arrived at home, it was quiet, but that was nothing new. *My husband is out,* I thought, *and Solange shut into her bedroom doing who knows what, planning her next revenge.* But when I passed by her door, I finally heard noises. I stopped and listened and could hardly believe my ears. Solange was moaning. What in God's name was happening? I hadn't thought her capable. And there was my husband, in a way I had only heard him be with me. Bedsprings were squeaking rhythmically.

I couldn't fathom it, but Solange and my husband were having sex. I had never heard someone else have sex before. What strangeness. Never in a million years would I have anticipated its happening like this if it was to happen at all. What had made Solange follow through on something to which she had never agreed, that had made her irate? Had I forced her, made her feel she must do it? Or was this revenge too? Or did it have nothing to do with me? Or . . .

I had every right to assert myself, yet ironically I felt

I was invading their privacy. I put my hand to the door as if I might knock, but only held it there gently and listened a while more.

Finally, I left them, walked upstairs to the bedroom I shared with my husband and fell back onto the bed. Almost without thinking, I began to touch my own body, and before long I felt my own pleasure. Immediately after, I burst out crying. It was sad to touch oneself in a moment such as this. It might even be pathetic. Or weird. I was weird.

I hadn't loved my husband, yet he probably hadn't loved me. It had obviously been easy for him to have sex with Solange, to do it while I was away, in the few hours in which I'd be gone from the house we lived in together. It was a cliché and I knew he didn't mind them, but I did.

Eventually he came upstairs to our room, where I lay reading. I wasn't crying any longer and didn't know if I should act angry. In that moment I really did hate him.

"What are you doing here? I thought you were seeing a play."

"I got sick."

"Oh." He nodded and seemed to consider this, then sat down in the chair at the foot of our bed.

"Is Solange a good lover?"

He looked up, but not at me. He was focused on a corner of the room. What he saw there I don't know. "You heard us?"

"I stood by the door listening for quite a while. It's possible I was there almost the entire time. I heard you cry out." I was lying, I hadn't heard everything, but I wanted him to think I had.

"There's no point in my denying it, then."

"You could try."

So he went on, "The men I play cards with—well, I came home, you can imagine it. I deserve a certain level of comfort from my wife. I didn't do anything, I promise, I just didn't stop it from happening. I'll have to go away for a few weeks and I was preparing for that. Solange will be let go. I won't allow things to get away from me here. I was dictating to my secretary; you see she has been a great help to me—I don't think I could do without her, you understand. You've never met my secretary and I don't know why that is. She asks about you often. I imagine you understand; you've always seemed like a very understanding person. Many men have told me many times. And yet, life goes on. I never thought I would experience it, but there was a presence in one of the other rooms, and then I felt that I had no control over my limbs, that something was moving me there. You seem as though you've often been moved against your will, so I would think you'd be able to relate to this. Women, I know they're attuned to something, they're always tuned in, I guess. I've often felt that women were tuned in to things they have no business being tuned in to. But you can't stop it, can you? Not you. You encourage it, in fact! Don't do that! But I wanted it, yes—I won't deny it. Women like me and I like women. My secretary brings me great comfort. And then I deserve comfort at home. I don't even like sex! But I do like comfort. Men told me. Why didn't I listen? And just who are you, anyway? Just what are you attuned to? I've only wanted to live a normal life, and with you that's impossible. Do you know what people say about you? Do you have any idea? They feel sorry for me! And now I know why. Please do not listen to my private moments. I am at home and I'll have what I want. You're like an old piece of pie I can't throw away, a very good pie. But I rescued you. You know that! And yet, I'd never seen anyone so alluring. You're always turning away. Turn toward me. Haven't you ever felt yourself carried away? Toward a woman? Something carried me to that room. Look at me, you are my wife, first and foremost, and I will be loyal to you. Let's go away, I'll take you to Brazil after all. Let me take you somewhere. Imagine it. We'll walk up and down the avenues. I'll protect you and keep you close. I gave very dear things to you, many, many jewels. Everything you're wearing right now. You are a proper woman. No, you are not. Clothes can't make a woman proper. Do you know how hard I've tried? And to be honest, I lay down on the bed—I did nothing else. I was exhausted. I don't think you realize how hard I work—not once have you come to my office!"

That is where I stopped listening. A part of me was floating. The room was a ship and I was already floating away. Where I was floating to I can't say, but it was mine, and his voice was becoming more and more distant. I hadn't actually thought that was possible.

W E DIDN'T SAY MUCH in the days that followed. My husband rambled no longer. It was all now back inside his head and body. Without drawing attention to myself, I began to prepare what I would take with me when I left. At night I let the dog and the cat sleep on the bed with me, which my husband had never allowed. He slept in one of the guest rooms. Solange avoided me as well, and I didn't know how to feel about her now that it was done. It was as if we were all at a silent retreat together, except for the negative energy. When I wrote in the evenings, the house was completely still.

I wrote about a painting I thought matched the situation.

*The interior is nearly colorless, a light gray room with light moldings, the room beyond gray as well, but darker, with small lamps of gold. The curtain that separates the two rooms is bright red. Three figures are dressed brightly too. A nobleman in green with a gold turban on his head. Two women dressed in saris of orange and yellow. The first woman holds the nobleman back at arm's length, and the*

*other woman covers her mouth in disbelief. Or perhaps it's*
*amusement. All of it is in miniature.*

Finally, my husband came to me for a talk. He told me I should leave. I had been expecting it.

"Where will I go?" I said innocently enough. "I have no money and no prospects for a job."

"I'll give you money, enough to live on. You won't be rich, but it's the least I can do. In exchange, we'll tell people that you refused to have a child, that you're unstable."

"But I'm not unstable."

"That remains to be seen."

I turned to the suitcase I had already been packing and folded one of my blouses before placing it inside. I was getting everything I wanted.

T HAT DAY I FINISHED PACKING, and by evening I was ready with what I would need in the weeks ahead, including the dog, who I had decided I was taking with me. The rest I would send for once I had found a place to live. When I left, Solange was nowhere to be seen, yet I saw her watch me from the door when I turned back to look one last time at the house. We stared at each other quite awkwardly, yet in the most direct look we had ever had.

Ironically, Solange had done what I wanted, all while leaving me completely in the dark. In a way, she had deceived me. Even in the transfer of my husband, she had refused any kind of partnership. I had not been able to know her, or perhaps I now did. Maybe I had been naïve. The beautiful house I had come to feel at home in was no longer mine; I assumed it would be hers from this point forward. How quickly things could change. Yet I had wanted it.

First I went to Antoinette's, where I stayed for the night, wide-awake while little Frederick cried. I felt lost in the sounds he made, but it wasn't entirely bad. When Antoinette got up to comfort him, she comforted me too. She sang Frederick his lullabies.

The next day I went to Dana's to tell her what had happened, but I couldn't stay over. Her family couldn't know yet that I was leaving. It was one of my husband's stipulations.

"Vitória, you're free," she said. "He's so stupid. He fell for it right away, and now he has to give you money." She pulled me tightly to her.

"I know." I was finally genuinely happy, even if a little nervous about my future. Then I pulled away. "Should I feel guilty?"

"No, of course you shouldn't. You deserve your freedom. People hardly ever get it." She shook me lightly. "Do you understand?"

I was being returned to something. "Yes. Yes, I'm free."

N ow I'm not far from home, but far enough for life to feel different, to be in the midst of strangers and, when I think of knowing them, to feel repelled. I know I shouldn't be that way toward another.

If I'm bored, at least it's not coming from outside my own life. I chose the boredom I'm a part of. In the mornings I write and then I look out at a field, imagining someone else's life. What it must be to look at this field forever. To farm it or to be the one who cooks all the meals.

Sometimes I am immersed in my writing, ecstatic; sometimes I am only able to write one paragraph. On certain days I hate that paragraph.

I look at my books of paintings while sitting at my desk. I look at paintings with snow in them. Here, people are skating across a pond, buying things from a Christmas market. How rosy they look. I don't think I've ever looked that rosy before.

Who am I if I'm not writing? I'm a person in a dance class, then I'm walking next to a dump. I listen to music, write my own name in my notebook, winter charging toward me. For things do charge, you must feel that too.

*The sky is flat against the mountains. The mountains and then the ground. Here is the place where the town turns into the country, and then the valley leading to the mountains, all of it the same piece of land. Here is a black dog, running wildly toward it all with all of its being. The last time I mirrored something I was coming to nature. Now I seem to be mirroring this dog.*

Still in the process of becoming, the soul makes room.

## ACKNOWLEDGMENTS

I would like to express my appreciation to Amanda Montei at *P-QUEUE*, Meghan Lamb at *The Spectacle*, and Nathaniel Klein and Brody Albert from Office Hours Gallery in Los Angeles (and curators of *The Mountain Show*), who published excerpts of this novel, sometimes in different form.

Short passages from Jean Rhys's *Wide Sargasso Sea*, Jean Genet's *The Maids*, and Octavia Butler's *Kindred* appear here, and I've named my characters after characters in those works, as well as Clarice Lispector's *The Apple in the Dark*. A passage also appears from *Goya: The Witches and Old Women Album*.

Thank you to my husband and best friend, Amarnath Ravva, for talking through the novel with me and for sharing your writing with me too.

Thank you to my parents, Deborah Miner and Steven Cain, for always having been encouraging and supportive, of writing and everything.

Thank you to Sofia Samatar and Anna Moschovakis, for reading early drafts of the novel and giving me such good and generous feedback, and for your own writing, to which I feel great kinship.

Thank you to Danielle Dutton, Kate Zambreno, Renee Gladman, Suzanne Scanlon, Bhanu Kapil, and Patty Cottrell. My work, including this novel, has been changed by reading yours, and I feel a kind of conversation with you when I write.

Thank you to Beth Nugent and Phyllis Moore. I don't think I've told you properly how special and invaluable you were as teachers when writing was still very new to me.

Thank you to my yoga teachers present and past, especially Samantha Jones Garrison, Adriana Rizzolo, Satyajeet Avila, Jessie Barr, Amanda Perri, Puja Singh Titchkosky, Camille Dieterle, Rachel Scandling, Ana Maria Delgado, and Sam Bianchini. I've learned so much from you, and sometimes parts of the novel came to me unexpectedly in your classes.

Thank you to my friends, especially Adam Novy, Daniel Borzutzky, Alicia Scherson, Richard Yoo, Adrienne Walser, Brent Armendinger, Ravish Momin, Alex Guthrie Branch, Laida Lertxundi, and Nathanäel.

With endless gratitude to my kind and wonderful agent, Mel Flashman. And to my editor Jeremy M. Davies, whom I have been lucky to work with, and whose sharp eyes have helped me make this novel better than it was before, somehow more itself. And thank you to everyone else at FSG.

A NOTE ABOUT THE AUTHOR

Amina Cain is the author of two collections of
short fiction, *Creature* and *I Go to Some Hollow*.
Her essays and short stories have appeared in
*n+1*, *The Paris Review Daily*, *BOMB*, *Full Stop*,
*VICE*, *The Believer Logger*, and other places. She
lives in Los Angeles and is a literature contributing editor at *BOMB*.